Next-Door Neighbours

Next-Door Neighbours

SARAH ELLIS

A Groundwood Book
Douglas & McIntyre
VANCOUVER/TORONTO

Groundwood Books
Douglas & McIntyre Limited
26 Lennox Street, Third Floor
Toronto, Ontario M6G 1J4

Canadian Cataloguing in Publication Data

Ellis, Sarah
    Next-door neighbours.

ISBN 0-88899-084-7

I. Title.

PS8559.L44N49 1989   jC813'.54   C89-093419-3
PZ7.E44Ne 1989

Cover illustration by Paul Zwolak
Design by Michael Solomon
Printed and bound in Canada

For Dad

1

PEGGY sat on a packing case, chewing a dry cheese sandwich and swilling Coke from a bottle. The bottle dripped water onto her shorts and the slivery wood of the packing case tickled the back of her knees. Coke for dinner was the most peculiar thing in a most peculiar day.

Candles set in foil tart plates lit the centre of the room. In the warm flickering light Peggy watched Mum cutting cheese with Colin's bowie knife and piling it on the slices of store-bought white bread that dominoed out of their plastic bag. Dad was kneeling on the floor pumping up gas in the camp stove. Colin was packing away his third cheese sandwich, and Dorrie was reading the phone book by candlelight. Nebuchadnezzar the cat was prowling the edges of the room, refusing to settle or be petted. The hiss and pop of the camp stove was the only sound. No, it wasn't, Peggy corrected herself. Under it was the quiet roar of what she realized was the city, their new home.

"Dorrie, what are you looking for? We can't use the phone yet. It isn't connected. Just like the electricity," Mum said with a sigh.

"I know. But there's nothing else to read. My books weren't put in my room." Dorrie frowned into the candlelight and went back to reading the directions for long distance phone calls. She had been in charge of labelling the moving boxes, and she had devised an elaborate system of organization. But the movers had not paid any attention.

They had loaded and unloaded the truck as the spirit moved them. Peggy had enjoyed watching them as they twirled the couch around, drank beer, made jokes and sang "There is nothing like a dame." But Dorrie was grumpy about the confusion.

The first disaster of the disaster-strewn day had been the movers arriving four hours late in the morning because their truck had broken down. Then Dad got lost and the cat threw up in the car and the new house wasn't ready for them and it all added up to the Davies family sitting in their new home at eleven o'clock at night with nothing unpacked, drinking Coke for dinner.

Outside the pool of candlelight in the dark corners of the room stood furniture and boxes. The furniture looked both familiar and strange. The uncurtained windows were squares of blackness. But outside it wasn't really dark, not like the country. There was a glow in the air.

The battered pot on the camp stove began to steam. "Now all we need are some cups," said Mum.

"Dishes have purple tape," mumbled Dorrie.

"I think the purple tape fell off in the move," grinned Colin, upending another Coke.

Dad took a candle off to the kitchen, disappearing into the blackness. His voice boomed out, " 'Many brave hearts are asleep in the deep, so beware. Be-ee-ee-ee-ware.' Peggy! Come hold the candle." Peggy meandered around the packing cases and furniture in the living room and the dining room. It felt as big as a church. There was a swinging door into the kitchen.

"Is this purple?" Dad asked, holding the candle next to a large box.

"I think so," said Peggy.

Dad flipped open the lid. Peggy reached in. It was like the lucky dip at the Christmas bazaar.

"Pay dirt!" said Dad as he unwrapped a teacup.

8

"But, Dad, it's one of the good cups."

"Any port in a storm, Pegeen, any port in a storm."

Peggy noticed that as everyone else was getting more and more tired, Dad was getting louder and livelier, more and more Dad-ish. Somehow the move had made everyone more themselves. Dorrie became very serious and organized, taping up check-lists and schedules and colour-coding everything in sight. Colin took advantage of the confusion to get exactly what he wanted, like buying a case of Coke at the corner store when Mum had sent him out for milk. Dad seemed to get larger and louder, exchanging jokes and songs with the movers, racing around the new house exclaiming at its wonders. Mum always said it was a good thing that Dad was a minister, because for at least a few hours a week, in church, he couldn't bounce.

And Mum smoothed out the wrinkles as usual, jollying people out of bad moods, finding lost things, cheering up Dorrie and toning down Colin and Dad. And what about me, wondered Peggy. Am I more myself over this move than usual? Am I more . . . ? She couldn't think of a single adjective to describe herself. Except, at the moment, tired.

Mum made tea right in the cups and in the darkness Peggy didn't notice the tea leaves until she felt them on her teeth.

"Where are we going to sleep?" asked Dorrie. "I don't think the movers put the beds in the right rooms."

"It's worse than that," said Dad. "You haven't been upstairs, but all the mattresses are on the landing."

"In a pile?" asked Peggy, thinking of the Princess and the Pea.

"No. Spread all over, like a carpet," said Dad.

Mum stood up. "I don't think I'll ever get used to how big this house is. Come on, then. A search for sheets and then we're all going to bed."

"On the landing?" asked Dorrie.

"On the landing," said Mum in a firm voice.

The sheets were finally found in a box marked with a yellow triangle. And then Colin washed his feet because Dorrie said she wouldn't sleep anywhere near him unless he did, and Colin and Peggy experimented with flushing the two toilets at the same time. Having two bathrooms was a novelty. They brushed their teeth with water because the toothpaste was nowhere to be found and settled in with sheets and coats over them because nobody could find the blankets. Nebuchadnezzar finally settled down and found his usual spot on Peggy's chest with his head tucked under her chin. Silence descended.

Then suddenly they all woke up again. Dad started it. "You know that mover called Paddy? The skinny one with the cowboy boots? Well, he told me that he's got this plan to go upcountry and buy himself a sawmill. What a character. Got to admire a young fellow like that. Just wants a sawmill of his own so he's going to do it. That's the spirit of the pioneers for you." Dad was always discovering all about people's lives. Five minutes and he knew all about their families and their dreams. Peggy, who could never think of a single thing to say to people, found this amazing.

"Right, Gareth," said Mum, "now that's really enough. We have a lot to do tomorrow."

But they couldn't stop. "Yellow-bellied sapsucker," said Colin into the darkness. Peggy exploded into giggles. In the long drive from the country they had played a game invented by Colin for making ordinary words sound rude.

"Reach for the sky, you low-living participle," said Dad.

But finally the conversation petered out. Peggy reached over to Mum who lay beside her. "Hey, Mum."

"Murgf."

"Is this what refugees feel like?"

"Well, I suppose so," said Mum. "But we have a whole bunch of new people waiting to welcome us. We don't need to worry about that. Go to sleep now, Peggy."

But the whole bunch of new people was exactly what Peggy was worried about. A whole new church, a whole new crowd of people who would look at her and talk to her. She wished she could just go on forever like a refugee. She didn't understand why her family always wanted to meet new people.

And then there was school. Four weeks of school to get through before the summer holidays. Her stomach began to jump just thinking about it. Walking into a new classroom, being stared at. Oh, well. At least tomorrow was Saturday, so she had two days before she had to face it. She lay in the warm spring night listening to her family breathing all around her.

2

T HE next morning Peggy woke to the feeling of the large, unknown house. She longed to explore, but everyone else wanted a real breakfast, and that meant hunting for the toaster and the kettle. It wasn't until mid-morning that Mum gave her the go-ahead.

She took a bottom-to-top approach, starting with the basement. It was larger than the basement at home. No, wait, she caught herself, this *is* home. But otherwise it wasn't very interesting, a wringer-washer and two grey sinks, lines for drying clothes, a can cupboard, a mysterious octopus-like furnace and a workshop. The walls of the workshop were covered in plywood on which someone had drawn the outlines of tools. An organized person, thought Peggy, like Dorrie. I wonder if it was the family before us or the family before them. Everybody leaving their mark, like ancient civilizations built one on top of the other.

She felt even more like an archaeologist when she discovered the marks on the basement door frame. Little notches at different heights and names scratched into the wood. "Michael — 1949, Christopher — 1951, Sally — 1954." The names leapfrogged up the door, ending up with "Michael — 1956" scratched almost higher than Peggy could reach. At knee level was one lone mark. Peggy pushed open the heavy squeaky door to get more light. "Bowser — 1951, 1952, 1953, 1954." She went back to the workbench and found a nail. She stood with her back to the door frame and pivoted the nail across the top of her head, marking the wood. "Peggy — 1956," she scratched beside it.

On the main floor Peggy started counting rooms. But it was hard to know what was a room. The front hall, for example, was so big that it certainly could count as a room, but its only purpose seemed to be to lead somewhere else. Besides, it could be divided into two with a heavy green velvet curtain that pulled across it. Good for plays, thought Peggy. From a point at the centre of the hall she could see four different wallpaper patterns — stone covered in ivy, maroon and grey stripes, ivory blobs on a beige background and antique cars. She wondered if one family had made all the choices.

The big rooms were almost like outdoors, making you want to run. But the small places were even better. A tiny cloakroom near the front door, the long, dark, sloping cupboard under the stairs, two lidded seats on either side of the fireplace. Perfect places for hiding.

There were two staircases going up to the second floor — one with dark wood bannisters leading up from the hall, and a narrow one from the kitchen. Peggy tried both routes and experimented with sliding down the bannister.

The second floor was busy with the activity of mattress moving, with Dorrie as bossy foreman and Colin as reluctant labourer. Peggy decided to delay a thorough look at her own room with its perfect forget-me-not wallpaper. She headed up to the attic.

It was bare and full of sunbeams, one big open room with windows at both ends and a sloping ceiling that came down to the floor. Peggy measured its length in cartwheels. Six cartwheels long. The bare wood floor gave her a sliver on the fifth turn. As she sat trying to remove the end of the sliver with her teeth, she noticed a door in the floor. She grabbed the iron ring and pulled hard. It opened abruptly. Sunlight streamed up. Peggy lay on the floor and stuck her

13

head down the hole. She found herself looking onto the outdoor porch that was off her own bedroom. A ladder was built into the wall. A trapdoor. Best thing of all.

She imagined lying in this attic room in the middle of the night, hearing a small squeak and seeing the trapdoor open slowly, slowly, slowly. By the third slowly Peggy had made it too real, and she tossed the image out of her mind, jumping up and lowering herself down the hole as her feet found the rungs of the ladder. She jumped down the last five rungs, went through the door into her own room-to-be, did somersaults across the mattresses still on the landing and ran up to the attic again.

She pushed open the window at the top of the stairs. To her right, over a gently sloping roof, was the back of the church hall. A movement in the garden to the left caught her eye. A small Chinese man in a white shirt and grey pants was hoeing down a green row. Peggy watched his rhythmical progress until he disappeared behind a shed.

From far away, two floors below, Mum called, "Lunchtime!"

"Look, I've got a few phone calls to make," said Dad after lunch. "Who wants to come over to the church with me?"

"I do, I do," said Peggy, seeing an escape from unpacking.

"Me too," said Mum. "I'd like a chance to have a look at the church while people are not having a look at me."

The Davies family had only visited the church once, several months before, when Dad had been invited to preach a guest sermon. Later Peggy realized it had been a sort of audition. All she remembered of the church was that it was big and had very old dark pews.

When they arrived, Mum and Dad both went into the office, leaving Peggy alone. Sun was streaming through the windows and, big as it was, the church had a familiar, friendly, Saturday-morning feel. It was a much grander

14

building than the church in the country, but it had the same smell of wood and dust and brass polish. It had many decorations that Peggy wasn't used to — golden organ pipes, some twice as tall as she was, a red glass lamp hanging in a side chapel, a glowing brass eagle holding the Bible on his outstretched wings. There was thick red carpet up the centre aisle. But the best things were the windows. Their old church had had coloured windows in little diamonds, but this one had pictures. One with fishermen, one with Jesus looking like a Sunday school teacher surrounded by children, and one surprising one with a boy scout. He didn't really look like a boy scout, more like a saint dressed up as a boy scout.

Peggy walked up the centre aisle and up the stairs into the pulpit. Standing there she felt powerful and full of knowledge and goodness. Saturday mornings in their old church, after her dusting, she had sometimes climbed into the pulpit and pretended to preach a sermon.

She looked out over the rows of empty pews below. She flipped over the pages of the Bible, ran her finger down the whisper-thin paper and stopped at random.

'' 'And I this day weak, though anointed king.' How often haven't we felt this way? We wake up in the morning and we feel weak.'' Peggy spoke very softly, just under her breath. But her gestures were expansive. She pointed grandly at the Bible. ''But as we can see from the Bible, even kings feel this way. Even,'' — pause for dramatic effect — ''the Prime Minister of Canada probably feels this way. And things weren't easy back in Bible times, either. Sometimes fishermen came back with empty nets, and they had plagues and locusts.'' She wiggled her fingers in the air to show things falling from the sky. ''Why, I myself last week woke up and felt I was getting a cold.'' Peggy leaned forward across the pulpit to share this personal anecdote, and as she did she glanced down.

15

Yikes! There, right in the front row, sitting quietly and looking up at her, was a strange boy. Without a thought Peggy ducked down behind the pulpit. Embarrassment weakened her knees and buzzed in her head, tilting the world in one dizzy moment.

Then she heard the side door open.

"Well, hello there," said Mum.

"Hello," said the boy's voice. "I'm George."

"Of course, George Slobodkin. The caretaker's son." Mum's voice got closer. "Have you met . . ." Mum came level with the pulpit stairs. She looked up and her eyes met Peggy's. "Good heavens, Peggy. What are you doing there?"

"Um. Looking for something I dropped."

Mum looked entirely unfooled. "Oh, yes. Anyway, come on out and meet George."

Peggy stood up, dusted off her knees and walked down the stairs. She didn't look at George.

"Hi."

"Hi, Peggy. I'm happy to meet you. Mr. Kelly, who was here before? His children were all too old to be friends with me. I was eager for you to arrive. We live in the basement. Are you going to be at Lord Nelson School? That's my school. What grade are you in? I'm in grade five. Do you want to come over to play?"

Peggy looked out from under her eyebrows at George. He was wearing black pants and a white long-sleeved shirt, all buttoned up to the neck. He looked strange, like a little man.

"Peggy?" Mum prompted.

"Yeah, I'll be at Lord Nelson School, in grade six. I don't think I can play, though. Not today."

George's face lost some of its brightness.

"Thanks, anyway," Peggy mumbled.

"Oh, yes, you'll be busy with the moving," said George. "But I'll see you tomorrow morning. Are you going to be in the junior choir? I'm a chorister myself."

Chorister? This kid talked weird. "I don't know. Maybe."

"Okay. Goodbye, Mrs. Davies." And George went out the back door.

Mum put her hand on Peggy's shoulder and steered her over to a side pew. It was the grip of an angry mother.

"Now what was that all about?"

"I don't know."

"Really. I was quite ashamed of you. Such a nice friendly youngster and you with not a word to say for yourself."

How could Peggy explain? "But, Mum, he was looking at me."

"Of course he was. He was interested in you. His mother told me he has been looking forward to us coming for weeks."

"But I can't think of things to say when people look at me like that." Peggy felt Mum's crossness spark her own homesickness, and tears welled up in her eyes. "You're mad."

"Oh, Peggy. Look. I know you're shy, though I thought you had gotten over it. But tomorrow is our first Sunday and we'll be meeting lots of new people. When you go all stiff and withdrawn like that it looks as though you're stuck-up and unfriendly. I know that you're not, so I don't want other people to think so. Will you try?"

"All right."

"Maybe it would help if you just concentrated on the person you were talking to, not yourself. Remember that a lot of the parishioners at this church are elderly. They probably don't have a chance to see many children, and it gives them a lot of pleasure. Anyway, enough said. Why don't you go home. I'll be back in a few minutes."

Peggy searched among the boxes in the hall until she found one labelled with a blue diamond that meant books. She slid her hand in under the flap and pulled out the top one.

It was a collection of household hints. Sigh. But, "any port in a storm, Pegeen," she told herself, and took it outside.

She lay under the peach tree in the backyard and read about how to keep ice-cube trays from sticking and how to use coat hangers to make useful and decorative gifts. She thought about what Mum had said and wondered if Mum had ever in her whole life felt shy. She guessed not. No one who had ever felt it could think that it came from being self-centred. It was exactly the opposite. When Peggy felt shy, it was as though her self abandoned her — as though the real Peggy rose up out of her body and hovered in the air, like an angel, looking down on the body-Peggy all frozen and stuttering. This angel-Peggy sometimes felt sorry for the body-Peggy, but she couldn't do anything to help.

And then that other thing that Mum always said. "Be yourself." What self did she mean? The brave one who swung out over the gully behind the school on a willow branch and fell and broke her leg just because it was a dare? Or the timid one who threw up when she had to go and sell Girl Guide cookies outside the supermarket? The noisy one who liked to play "Chopsticks" on the piano with the loud pedal on? Or the quiet one who liked to find a hidden place to go and read?

It was all very difficult. Peggy looked up "shyness" in the index to her book, but there was nothing between "Shower curtains, mildew on," and "Stain removal, table of."

I guess there's no household hint for this problem, she thought.

3

SUNDAY turned out to be better than Peggy had expected. They didn't have to talk to anyone before church, because they were almost late. A bottle of Dorrie's perfume, unaccountably packed in among Colin's shirts, had broken in the move, and Colin refused to go to church smelling like "Eau de Shalimar." Finally he agreed to wear one of Dad's shirts, but then he had to wear a jacket to hide his rolled-up sleeves.

They hurried in the front door of the church just before the choir started up the main aisle. Peggy felt all eyes on them as they paraded in, but then it was the service, and nobody was supposed to stare during church. She looked at the leaflet to see the number of the first hymn and her name jumped up at her: "This Sunday the people of St. Jude's are pleased to welcome their new rector, the Rev. Davies and his wife and family, who come to us from St. Peter's Church, Cedargrove. The Davieses have three children: Doreen, 17, Colin, 16, and Margaret (Peggy) 12."

During the sermon Peggy noticed George looking at her from the choir stalls at the front, and she guessed that he was remembering her performance yesterday. After that she kept her eyes glued on the hat of the old lady in front of her. It was decorated with a veil and a long pheasant feather pointing upwards. As the lady shifted, the tip of the feather bounced in the air.

After church there was a welcoming tea. This was just the sort of event that Peggy found torture. Faces loomed. Ladies smelling like face powder, hearty bluff men in suits who patted her head with big hands, kids of her own age who flashed her that "prove it" look.

Peggy went to stand beside Dad. He was still wearing his long cassock and she remembered how, when she was little, she used to pull it around her and hide in its folds. She wanted to now. The lady in the feather hat was talking to Dad, ignoring the line of people that was forming behind her.

"Peggy, this is Mrs. Manning," Dad said. "She's our next-door neighbour."

Mrs. Manning leaned over and examined Peggy through her veil. "How lovely to have children in the rectory again. You must come and visit me often."

She swept away leaving a ghost of flowery perfume.

The other adults in the line-up mostly asked the same questions: "How old are you?" (Didn't they read the leaflet? Peggy wondered) and "How do you like life in the city?" The first time this was asked, Peggy tried to answer truthfully. A chasm of conversational possibility opened up before her. She thought about how it didn't get really dark at night, or totally quiet. She thought about the trap door and the back staircase. But by the time she had sorted through these ideas, it was too late. So she just took to saying either, "It's nice," or "It's different."

But in comparison to other events of the sort, Peggy felt she survived pretty well. Colin, in one of his rare moments of big brother kindness, stuck right by her, rescuing her when her tongue tied in knots and whispering rude things in her ear between conversations. "A pox on you, you wide mouth Mason jar."

George brought them a plate of goodies when they got trapped by Major Somebody-or-other who told Colin how splendid it would be if he joined the army cadets. Peggy realized that George wasn't going to give her away about the incident in the pulpit and she felt a flicker of gratitude. But then he asked her if she wanted to walk to school the next day, and she panicked. Imagine walking to school with a boy, and a grade five boy at that, and a grade five boy with funny clothes, even worse. She grasped at a lifeline. ''No, sorry. My mum has to come with me the first day.''

But if Sunday wasn't too bad, Monday was another story. At nine o'clock Mum walked down the hill with Peggy and they went into the big brick building. They were shown into the principal's office and Mum handed over Peggy's school records from Cedargrove and they filled in forms.

''I think she'll be very happy in Mrs. Bristow's grade six class,'' said the principal. ''And welcome to the community, Mrs. Davies.'' Then Mum left and Peggy had a sharp-edged memory of how it had felt when Mum had left her the first day in grade one, a sense of complete abandonment.

When she walked into Mrs. Bristow's class Peggy felt eyes boring into her. Through the roaring in her ears she heard snatches of Mrs. Bristow's welcome and then she sank gratefully into her seat. She fixed her eyes firmly on the arithmetic questions on the blackboard.

When the girl sitting in front of her went to the board, Peggy recognized her. She had met her the day before at the church tea. Her name was Linda and she had long red hair in braids, pale skin and freckles. She smiled at Peggy when she returned to her seat. Peggy tried to get her face ready to smile back, but she didn't quite make it before Linda sat down.

When the recess buzzer rang, Peggy let herself be carried out into the hall with the crush. Glancing down the grey corridor with its lines of bulletin boards, she spotted a washroom sign. She fled there and locked herself in a cubicle. She didn't have to go. She pulled her feet up onto the seat and tied and retied each shoe twice. She listened to the girls come and go, running water, flushing toilets, talking, giggling. Then she looked at her watch. Ten minutes left to go.

She thought about Mum's advice. Be yourself. Okay, the inside voice was firm, I'll go out onto the playground and if I see Linda I'll just go right up and say, "Hi. I'm Peggy. I met you yesterday." Twice she practised her line, trying to sound casual, friendly and, above all, herself.

She walked out the front door of the school and paused on the edge of the schoolyard. She felt as conspicuous as someone with green skin. Sure enough, there was Linda at the centre of a knot of girls and taller than most of them. She's popular, thought Peggy, her stomach sinking. I can't possibly go and talk to someone who is popular.

Just then she noticed George. He was walking alone across the field, tossing a ball in the air. It was a red, white and blue rubber ball like the ones the primary girls were bouncing against the school wall. In his little man clothes he looked weird. He noticed Peggy, grinned, and veered toward her. That's all I need, thought Peggy. To be seen with a loser on my very first day. She glanced around. Linda's group was the only safe place. Taking a deep breath she approached them.

"Hi, Linda."

The circle opened and she walked in. Linda introduced everyone and Peggy forced herself to look each girl in the eye and smile, even though her face felt wooden. She concentrated on remembering their names — Jane, Louise, Elizabeth, Frances, Renate.

They were talking about horses. "I'd have a palomino," said the girl with rosy cheeks.

"Oh, Jane, you've been saying that since grade four."

"Well, so what? I still think they're the prettiest."

"I'd keep my horse in a stable down by the beach and every morning at dawn I'd ride it bareback along the edge of the waves," said a girl wearing a plaid headband. Louise?

"I had a horse."

The words dropped into the babble like a stone into a still pond. All eyes turned to Peggy.

"What?"

Peggy's mind was racing. She hadn't meant to say that. The lie had just dropped out of her mouth. But as soon as she did say it she could picture the non-existent horse. He was small and brown and friendly. She took a deep breath.

"Yes, when I lived in the country. I rode him to school."

"Wow!" The girls looked at her as though she was a movie star. "What was his..."

Bzzzzzzzzt. The school buzzer ripped through their conversation, and a gang of kids pushed through the group, crowding in the doors.

"Hey, Peggy, see you at lunch," yelled Jane, carried away on the tide of the crowd.

All through spelling, Peggy's brain kept flitting back to the horse. What had she done? She had told the biggest fib of her life. But how could she undo it? Stand there at lunchtime and say, "I didn't have a horse. I just made it up"?

I know, she thought. I'll just say no more about it. Everyone will forget and it won't matter.

But in social studies, which was a unit on climatic vegetation zones which they had already done at Cedargrove, she let her mind wander to the horse. He seemed so real. What would his name be? Star? Beauty? No — Fox. Because of his browny-red coat. As soon as he had a name Peggy could feel his velvety mouth nuzzling the palm of her hand and smell the dust on his curry comb. She felt him under her, trotting around a field and then gathering himself to break into a gallop. She saw herself on all-day trail rides with a saddlebag full of lunch, heading over the hills alone.

When the bell rang for lunch it was clear that nobody had forgotten about the horse. Linda whipped around in her seat and grabbed Peggy's arm.

"What colour was he?"

"Who?"

"Your horse."

"Oh, he was a sort of red-brown."

"And did you ride him to school every day?"

"Yes. He stayed outside and waited for me."

"Lunch, girls," said Mrs. Bristow, shooing them outside.

"Come on, Peggy," said Louise.

In the echoing lunchroom she found it remarkably easy to talk about Fox's stall and her saddle and the road to school. She made the most of her memories of the few trail rides she had taken and of the "Pony for Angela" series she had read. Part of her was terrified that she would be found out. But another part was sure she could survive this period of attention. Then the horse interest would die down and she could melt into the group and become herself again.

In the middle of describing riding Fox in the snow, Peggy caught sight of Linda looking a bit sour. She knew immediately what was wrong. Linda was used to being the centre of attention. Suddenly she felt trapped by her lie, sick of the whole subject of horses. She pulled a package of elastic bands from her pencil case. "Hey, anybody want to play Chinese Skip?"

They played Chinese Skip for the rest of lunch and Jane walked home with her after school and everything seemed okay. But behind the okayness was one large horse-shaped worry. And as soon as Peggy would begin to forget it, it would give a soft whinny to remind her that it was there.

4

L ATER in the week the horse-shaped worry was joined
by a cat-shaped worry. Nobody had seen Nebbie for
three days. On Thursday morning Peggy explored the bottom of her bed with her feet before she even opened her
eyes. No warm lump of cat. Cars swished by on the rainy
street. Nebbie wasn't used to lots of traffic.

At breakfast Mum said not to worry, that cats often went
into hiding after a move, just until they felt at home. The
new house certainly had lots of cat-sized hiding places, but
what was Nebbie eating?

Then Mum said something that drove all thoughts of
Nebbie away. She had been to a church women's group
meeting. "Well, I seem to have made my first major goof.
Apparently the Ladies' Fellowship always does the mid-
summer tea, but this year several of their key members are
away and they were worried that they couldn't manage it.
I don't blame them. They are very elderly. So I suggested
they combine forces with the Women's Guild. Well! *That*
met with a tense silence. And then I was asked in frigid
tones whether I wished to make that a motion. So of course,
I didn't. Afterwards when I was helping wash up the tea
things with Millie Hoskins, she told me all about it. You
see, apparently the two groups were one group in the past
and then there were *ructions* and part of the group broke
away, spear-headed by our next-door neighbour, Mrs. Manning. So now they are completely separate and never the

twain shall meet. By the way, Millie Hoskins has a grand-daughter in your grade, Peggy. Do you know her? Her name is Linda.''

Peggy nodded. ''She's in my class.''

Mum decapitated her boiled egg with a bold swipe of the knife. ''Anyway, I had a nice chat with Millie, who really is a dear. What odd ideas she has about the country, though. Somehow she had gotten it in her head that we all rode around on horses. They must think we lived on the old homestead or something.''

At the mention of horses, Peggy's heart plummeted. So. Linda had told her grandmother about Fox. And Mum had told Mrs. Hoskins that it wasn't true. And soon Mrs. Hoskins would tell Linda and Linda would know that Peggy had lied. Not wanting to go to school the first day was nothing compared to not wanting to go to school now.

Peggy tried to walk down the hill as slowly as possible, but it was pouring and the rain found a route into the collar of her yellow slicker and down her back. So finally, with a sigh, she opened the door to the girls' play area in the basement. It was warm and wet and her glasses steamed over. She took them off and stared into the blur. Linda's red hair was a bright patch in the corner, surrounded by a group of whispering girls. That's it, thought Peggy. They know about the lie and they're laughing at me. She turned to head out into the rain again when Louise bounced over.

''Peggy! Come here and see Franny's perm.''

Frances's head had expanded to about three times its usual size. Her hair stood all around in giant curls, like haloes around the heads of saints. ''It's a Toni,'' Frances said proudly. ''My mum and my aunt gave it to me. What do you think, Peggy?''

''I think it's great,'' said Peggy, which was half of what she thought. The other half was that it made Frances's head look too big for her body. Everybody went on chatting.

Nobody looked at Peggy in any strange way. They hardly looked at her at all. So, she was safe for another day. But it was like sitting on a time bomb. How often did Linda visit her grandmother? If she could just hold out for three more weeks until the end of school, it would be all right. Next September was too far away to worry about.

After school Peggy decided to walk into the house just as though Nebbie wasn't missing. She opened the front door and paused for a minute, waiting for a black streak to bounce down the stairs and thread itself around her legs. No cat. She went into the kitchen and opened a drawer. She took out a spoon and tapped the counter in a cat-food sort of way. She stepped out onto the back porch and called, "Nebbie-Nebbie-Nebbie-Nebbie," until her tongue got twisted. No cat. Only Colin who came out from under the porch carrying a greasy rag.

"Still no cat? We should go and look for him," he said.

"What do you mean?"

"I've got the bike working now, and since the rain has finally let up I want to go for a run and test a few things out. Why don't you come along and we'll see if we can find Nebbie around the neighbourhood?"

"Sure! Just wait while I change." Peggy ran up to her room and changed into play clothes. She scribbled a note to Mum. In the backyard the motorcycle snarled and ripped. The dogs across the alley began a wild barking.

By the time she got back to the yard, Colin had toned down the engine to a rhythmical *putt-putt* punctuated by the odd throat-clearing sound from the innards. Peggy jumped on the back, placed her feet on the pedals and held on properly to the strap that was fixed across the seat. But as soon as Colin started up the bumpy alley, she grabbed him around the waist and squished her head against his back.

They rode up and down streets and alleys. Once every block Colin stopped and they called out for Nebbie. They saw lots of cats. Sprawled, arched, asleep, streaking across streets. Smoke-coloured, ginger, marmalade, dirty white and clean white. They even saw some black cats. But not one with two white paws and a white moustache. Not one that came when they called. Not one named Nebuchadnezzar Davies.

After an hour Peggy's head ached with the noise of the motorcycle, and Colin was fed up with stopping so often. They decided to quit. "Let's just drive around the park before we go home," said Colin, "so we can get up some speed."

On the five-mile spin Peggy clung to Colin's back like a barnacle. The wind whipped by her ears and through her hair. She could feel Colin's chest vibrating. She knew he was singing but she couldn't hear a word. She loosened her arms slightly so that she could look up as they drove under the trees that formed a green arch over the road. She gripped her knees to the seat and pretended she was on a horse.

On the way back home they passed by the school. Jane and Linda were there skipping. Peggy almost waved, thinking how surprised they would be, but shyness overcame her. They bounced up the rocky alley and came to a halt in the backyard. Colin stretched his arms up to the sky and yelled, "Whoopee!" Peggy leaned back, letting her feet slide off the pedals and her legs dangle down.

Suddenly a searing pain shot up from her right leg. She gave a sharp hiccup of surprise and then a scream. She half-fell, half-jumped onto the ground. Colin was instantly beside her, pushing over the motorcycle as he jumped. "Peggy, Peggy. What is it?"

Peggy's whole self was concentrated on a six-inch strip of pain on the inside of her right leg. She couldn't look. She could only roll back and forth. "My... leg."

The back door crashed and Mum was beside her. Her voice and Colin's were distant and disjointed. "Peggy, darling. Colin, what happened?... The muffler? Colin! This is red-hot. No wonder... . Get some cold water. Quick."

With the first splash of water on her leg, Peggy fainted. When she came to she was cradled in Mum's arms and Colin was pouring a steady careful stream of water from the watering can onto her leg. "More, Colin. The important thing is to cool it down as quickly as possible." The pain had dulled to a steady throb and Peggy twisted around to look at her leg. "Peggy, honey, are you okay?"

"I fainted."

"I know. That's a very nasty burn." Mum's face was white. "Oh, my, when I heard you scream like that I thought...I didn't know what to think."

"What happened?"

"It was the muffler on the bike." Colin's voice was very small. "It got really hot and when you put your leg there it burned it."

"Muffler?" said Peggy, still confused.

"This thing." Colin pointed to a shiny metal tube that ran along the side of the motorcycle. "Should I get more water?"

Mum looked down. Colin had poured so much water over Peggy's leg that all three of them were sitting in a shallow lake. Suddenly Mum began to laugh. "Oh," she half-choked. "I'm so sorry. It's just that I always — laugh in emergencies." Mum doubled over and then straightened up and looked at them again, her face controlled and serious. But it cracked after a second. And her laugh was contagious.

So when Dad looked out the church office window, he saw Mum holding Peggy and Colin both, all three sitting in a mud puddle and laughing their heads off.

It wasn't funny later though. Even with bags of ice cubes and being read to and a Fudgsicle from the corner store the pain just went on and on. There was only one way Peggy could lie in bed and keep her leg from touching the sheets, and as soon as she dozed off her body forgot and curled up into its usual curve. She slept and woke all night long.

In the morning the leg was fine if she lay perfectly still, but when she put it over the side of the bed it throbbed, and if she tried to put weight on it, electric arrows shot up and down.

"No school today," said Mum as she helped her hop to the bathroom.

Silver lining, thought Peggy. One more day she wouldn't have to face being found out.

Mum brought her extra pillows and lemonade with a straw. Colin moved his radio into her room. Dorrie provided a carefully catalogued and indexed collection of *Children's Digest*. But by noon she was entirely bored by stories of great men and their deeds, "The First Telescope," "Cities of Destiny" and Buster Bunny's lessons on sharing. She didn't want to see another dot-to-dot puzzle in her life and she didn't want to hear "Don't Be Cruel" ever again on the radio. She was counting the bunches of flowers on her wallpaper when Dad came in for lunch.

"Want to join me in the garden?" he asked. He set up a deck chair, a footstool and a little table for her under the peach tree and helped her hop down the stairs. On the way Peggy imagined being a cripple in an old children's book. She practised putting on a holy look until Dad asked her sympathetically if the pain was worse.

After lunch Dad renewed her ice-cube bag and went off hospital visiting. Mum made a new pitcher of lemonade and left for a meeting of the Mothers' Union. "I'm just going to smile and offer to make lemon tarts."

"You mean you're not going to suggest they merge with the Ladies' Fellowship?" said Peggy.

Mum looked at her sideways. "Better watch it, horrible child, or it will be the rack for you."

"No. No! Not the rack!" said Peggy, falling into the familiar routine. "Anything but the rack!"

"Anyyyyyything?" said Mum in a monster voice, pushing her nose right up against Peggy's.

"The rack. Please — the rack, the rack!"

Mum kissed her on the nose. "Home by three. Be good."

Peggy was lying in a half-doze, contemplating the dot-to-dot possibilities of the freckles on her arm, when she heard mewing. A faint and lonely sound. She sat straight up. "Nebbie? Nebuchadnezzar?" She strained to hear under the noise of the garbage truck in the alley. Again the faint cry of a cat floated across the garden. It seemed to be coming from next door. Peggy was half out of the deck chair before a flash of pain pushed her back into it. She breathed deeply until the wave retreated and then carefully lowered herself onto the grass. With one leg and two hands she inch-wormed her way toward the next-door hedge. She flipped over to a kneeling position and stuck her head through the leaves.

She was startled by a man who was working with a hoe just a few feet away. It was the Chinese man she had spied from the attic window that first day. She nearly pulled her head back but then she heard the tiny and persistent cry again.

"Did you hear that?" she asked the man.

He turned and smiled. A crow sitting on the telephone wire began scolding the world.

"That?" he asked.

"No. A cat. Listen."

They both waited in silence until Peggy began to think that she had dreamed the sound. Then she heard it again. "That. Hear it?"

"Yes. Coming from the house?"

"Oh," said Peggy, disappointment flooding through her. "It's your cat then."

"No. Mrs. Manning doesn't have a cat. I'll go and look."

The man walked to the house, down a few concrete steps and tugged on an old door that screeched as it opened. He disappeared into the blackness. Peggy pushed her head farther through the hedge and waited. Suddenly a black ball shot out of the door, streaked across the garden, jumped up on the fence and turned into Nebuchadnezzar. Two white paws, white moustache and all. He began to lick himself as though nothing had happened.

"Nebbie. Nebbie." Peggy pushed her way through the hedge, noticing but not caring that she scraped her leg as she did so, and flopped onto a row of seedlings. "Oh. Sorry."

Nebbie jumped in a graceful arc off the fence and walked daintily over to Peggy's lap. He left a sooty patch on her shorts. "Nebbie. Where have you been?"

The man emerged from the basement. "I found him in the coal bin. Locked in, I guess."

Peggy leaned over and rubbed her face in the cat's fur. Tears prickled her eyes. "We just didn't know where he was. We moved in and for a long time we thought he was hiding in the house because cats do that when they've just moved. And he's never moved before. He was born in our other house, just like me. And Colin, that's my brother, took me on his motorcycle and we looked all over the place for him and here he was all the time, just next door. Boy, am I glad he wasn't lost forever."

The man had picked up his hoe and was working again. Suddenly Peggy really looked at him. Oh, gosh. Here she was, sitting in the dirt with coal dust and tears on her face talking to a grownup that she didn't even know. She didn't even know his name. But now, oddly enough, it seemed too late to feel shy.

"What's the cat called?" the man asked.

"His real name is Nebuchadnezzar. It's from the Bible. Dad named him. But mostly we just say Nebbie or Nebbie-cat."

The man went on hoeing. He didn't seem to think that you needed to talk every second when you were having a conversation. He was also a glancer, not a starer. Peggy always felt uncomfortable with people that looked right into your eyes, as though they were trying to get in. She extended her palm and let Nebbie butt against it. She looked out from under her eyebrows at the man. He was wearing a white cotton shirt that was very neatly ironed. The line of his shirt met the line of his black hair like a geometry diagram. He was a very tidy hoer. Dig and pull, dig and pull, leaving a symmetrical scalloped line along the row.

He paused. "Where I worked before, for the Lane family, the cat got closed in the flour bin. When I opened the bin the cat came out. *Fwit!* Just like Nebbie. Flour all over the kitchen."

"How did he get in there?"

"This is what Mrs. Lane asked. All the children, six children in the Lane family, said they didn't know. But I think Daphne did it. Daphne — youngest child. Daphne did everything — ran away, cut her own hair, threw the governess's face powder out the bathroom window."

"Did she get in trouble?"

"Not for the cat in the flour bin, but lots of other trouble. Daphne was a very bad child."

From his smile and the warmth of his voice Peggy knew that he had really liked Daphne. She thought she might like her herself.

"Where is she now?"

"She is a grownup lady. Lives in Victoria, I think." He began another row.

"Tell me more about the governess."

Ting. Ting. The soft but definite sound of a bell came from inside the house. The man straightened up and propped his hoe against the hedge. ''I must go now. That is Mrs. Manning's bell.'' He brushed the dirt off his hands in a neat burst of applause and held out one hand to Peggy. ''Pleased to meet you. My name is Sing Lee.''

Peggy grasped the outstretched hand. It struck her funny to do the handshaking part of the conversation last. But better. Then you didn't have to worry about what to say when that part was over. ''I'm Peggy Davies. Thanks for, you know, rescuing Nebbie.'' Sing smiled and his eyes crinkled up, and then he was gone.

5

PEGGY'S leg stopped hurting so badly but she couldn't walk properly for four days. She spent the weekend sitting on a deck chair in the garden, being bored. She saw George twice, once when he was snapping out a dusting cloth from one of the church hall windows and once when he was dragging a garbage can into the alley. He grinned and waved both times.

Monday at noon Mum announced they were invited to Mrs. Manning's for afternoon tea.

"Aw, Mum, do I have to?"

"Yes," said Mum firmly. "She has invited us several times and she's particularly anxious for you to come."

Mrs. Manning's living room was dim and quiet and filled with bulky furniture. All the surfaces were covered. The tables and piano and mantle were busy with framed photos, vases of dried flowers, ivory elephants and china ornaments. The upholstered furniture was dotted with doilies. Dark paintings hid the walls. The whole room looked like a "Find the hidden objects" puzzle in *The Children's Digest*. A grandfather clock tocked slowly in the corner, and the air smelled old.

Peggy sat on the hard, slippery couch. Mrs. Manning questioned her about school and her accident. Then she gave her a wooden puzzle and an album of postcards. The puzzle was too easy and the postcards, page after page of lakes and waterfalls, were boring.

Peggy glanced at the grandfather clock. Recess time. She imagined school — a game of tag, the thwack of a lacrosse ball against the gym wall, the brush of skipping ropes and, in a corner by the auditorium door, a small group of girls gathered around Linda. "Guess who's a liar? Peggy Davies. That's who. That horse of hers is one big fib. My granny found out."

"Time for tea, I think," said Mrs. Manning, ringing a small bell that stood on the table beside her.

A few minutes later Sing came through the door, pushing a tea trolley laden with cups, a silver tea set, a plate of scones and a plate of cookies.

"Hi, Sing," said Peggy. Sing smiled and nodded.

"You've met, have you?" said Mrs. Manning.

"Yes," said Peggy, "in the garden."

"Well," Mrs. Manning paused, "isn't that nice?" She took the lid off the teapot and stirred vigorously. "Thank you, Sing. That will be all for the moment."

The scones and cookies both had raisins. Peggy had not been able to eat raisins since Colin had said they looked like dead flies. The tea was thick with real cream instead of the milk she was used to. Teatime took forever. Only Peggy's sore leg kept her from leaping down the stairs when they left.

By the next day Peggy could walk again, and she was relieved to hear Mum say she could go back to school. It would be better to be there facing the lie than at home dreading it. As she dressed, carefully pulling on her underwear to avoid touching her leg, she caught herself humming "Onward Christian Soldiers." She felt she was putting on her armour for battle.

It took longer than usual to walk the four blocks to school, so she arrived just as the five-minute buzzer sounded across the schoolground. In the line-up outside the class, Jane turned around and whispered, "How come you were away?"

"Burnt my leg."

"How?"

"On a motorcycle muffler."

"You ride a motorcycle!" Jane looked impressed. "Hey, Linda." She tugged one of Linda's braids. "Peggy burnt her leg on a motorcycle."

Linda turned around and stared directly at Peggy. "Too bad, Peggy. I didn't know you had a motorcycle as well as a horse."

"Oh, it's not mine. My brother..." Peggy's stomach turned over.

They stared at each other for a long second. Then Peggy dropped her eyes and began to search through her pencil case. Jane looked from one to the other and gave a nervous laugh. "Come on, Linda. Of course she doesn't own a motorcycle. Twelve-year-olds don't own motorcycles. It's her brother's. Have you seen him? He carries the cross in church. He's really cute." The buzzer blatted through her words and Mrs. Bristow opened the classroom door.

All through current events and spelling, Peggy stared at the back of Linda's head. She counted the bumps in each red braid. Maybe it was all right, she thought. Maybe I just imagined the sarcasm in her words.

But on the way out to recess Linda grabbed Peggy's arm and pulled her out of the surge. She didn't waste words.

"Listen. After recess there's an arithmetic test."

"Yeah." Peggy tried to sound tough but her voice squeaked. She cleared her throat and swallowed.

"We'll probably pass back to mark."

"So?"

"You'll be marking mine. I don't want to get any mistakes."

Peggy tried one final bluster. "I don't know what you mean."

Linda just stared at her. "You know what I mean." She gave Peggy a shove and ran off. "Hey, Frances. Wait up!"

Peggy spent recess reading a riddle book and explaining the blister on her leg to anyone who asked. Twice she thought about going to the school nurse and saying that her leg hurt. But she didn't. She had the feeling of sitting in a roller coaster, hearing the safety bar slam into place and feeling the first jerk of motion.

The arithmetic test wasn't hard, but Peggy couldn't concentrate. She got to the first step of reasoning how to compare two cars travelling down the highway at different speeds and then her mind wandered. She started again. She wasn't even halfway through the test when Mrs. Bristow called time.

"Back person to the front, everyone else pass backwards, please and thank you." Linda passed her paper around without turning to look at Peggy.

Please let her get them all correct, prayed Peggy, and then cancelled the thought. It didn't seem right to involve God in all this.

There were ten problems. Linda got the first three right. On the fourth her lightly pencilled answer, "Eight gallons," glared up at Peggy as Mrs. Bristow said crisply, "Eight quarts." Peggy put neither a cross nor a tick. She started to chew the inside of her cheek and missed what Mrs. Bristow said for question five.

She leaned over to Elizabeth and whispered, "What was the answer to five?"

"Problems, Peggy?" asked Mrs. Bristow.

"I missed the answer to five."

"Three hours, ten minutes," said Mrs. Bristow a bit crossly.

Peggy rubbed the word "gallons" with her finger. It would erase easily. Time was running out.

"Question nine. Mr. Brown's brick wall would be twice as high as Mr. Green's brick wall." Peggy ticked Linda's answer.

"And last but not least, number ten is seven-eighths. Robbie? Yes, all right, fourteen-sixteenths will do in this case. Front people collect the papers, please. No, you don't all need to turn around. I'll read out the marks."

Linda hadn't turned around.

Peggy flipped over her pencil and held the eraser above Linda's mistake. Then she twirled it back again, put a clear *x* next to question four and marked nine out of ten at the bottom of the paper in small neat figures.

Mrs. Bristow raised her eyebrows over the top of her glasses when she read out Peggy's mark, four out of ten. She made a little pleased noise when she read out Linda's. Peggy stared at her desk.

Linda didn't turn around during the rest of arithmetic or during silent reading. Several times Peggy almost tapped her on the shoulder. She didn't know what she was planning to say, but she could read the anger in Linda's back and she felt trapped.

It was hot dog day in the lunchroom, and everyone else raced out of the classroom as quickly as they could when dismissed. Peggy spent a long time putting her pencils and notebooks back in her desk. She was the last one out of the room and Mrs. Bristow was right behind her. Peggy felt the teacher's hand on her shoulder.

"Not to worry about the test, Peggy. You must just not be feeling well with that nasty burn."

Peggy's eyes filled with tears and she opened them wide. She had put on her armour for nastiness and teasing, but it dissolved at Mrs. Bristow's kindness. "Uh, I'm okay," she mumbled and headed off down the hall trying to look like a girl whose only worry was an arithmetic test.

In the lunchroom she bought a hot dog and a carton of milk and a long john doughnut. She answered the questions of the lunchroom mums about her leg. Then she turned the corner into the big room with all the tables. The grade six girls were in their usual spot. The first to catch Peggy's eye was Jane who gave her a quick glance, looked very embarrassed, and then turned away.

Peggy took a deep breath, balanced her doughnut more securely on top of her hot dog and headed over to the table. As she approached, Linda grabbed the one empty chair and pushed it, squealing along the floor, to the next table.

"We don't have room at our table," she announced. And everyone else adjusted their chairs to close the gap. Nobody really looked at Peggy. They all just moved in and began to whisper.

I don't care, said Peggy to herself, and the words gave her enough starch to look around for another seat before she became conspicuous. She sat down at the primary table and carefully opened her milk. Some of the little kids gave her curious glances, not unfriendly, but she stared away into the distance, trying to look as serene and grownup as possible. Luckily a blond boy named Marvin provided a distraction, printing his name on his hot dog in mustard. Because his full name was Marvin L. MacGregor, he used quite a bit. When he bit into the hot dog, mustard squooged out the sides of the bun all over his face. Squeals of delight from the primary table brought the lunchroom monitor over, and nobody paid any more attention to Peggy. She ate her hot dog without tasting it.

All afternoon nobody talked to her or even looked at her. She began to feel invisible. After school she only wanted to get home as quickly and quietly as possible. But George ran to join her as she trudged up the hill. He walked in an odd way, rising up onto the balls of his feet, giving a bounce on each step. He also carried a large heavy briefcase. As he swung it at the end of his outstretched arm, its weight jerked him forward a bit. Jerk and bounce. Jerk and bounce. Peggy looked around to make sure nobody was watching them.

Finally in annoyance she said, ''Why do you carry that?''

George grinned. ''Isn't it splendid? My father got it in the church rummage sale. Look.'' He crouched down on the grass boulevard and opened his briefcase. ''It has two compartments and a zipper part on this side and it even locks.'' He snapped it shut, took a key from around his neck and locked it. ''Pretty good, isn't it?''

''Nobody else carries a briefcase in grade five,'' said Peggy.

''I know. I guess nobody else found one in a rummage sale,'' said George happily. Jerk and bounce. Jerk and bounce. ''Peggy? Are we next-door neighbours?''

''What?''

''Next-door neighbours. Is that what we are?''

This George was really strange. What was he getting at? ''Well, we live next door to each other if that's what you mean. Why?''

''Great! Ever since we came to Canada I've wanted next-door neighbours. In the New Canadian class we had a book called *Next-Door Neighbours*, and it was the first book that I read in English. So I wanted next-door neighbours. But in the book they all have houses lined up on a street with big green lawns and fences. Because our door is on the lane I didn't know if you would count as my next-door neighbour.''

''*Next-Door Neighbours?* That's the reader we had in grade one. That's a baby book.''

''Oh, yes, but that's because we couldn't read hard books in English yet. Anyway I liked the family in that book.''

Peggy suddenly remembered her own joy in *Next-Door Neighbours*. The shiny blue cover and the way the soft pages felt as though they had baby powder on them. The fat black

41

letters, the happy smiling family with her favourite character, Rover the dog. Her pleasure at recognizing the word "something," the longest word in the book.

But she certainly wasn't going to share such thoughts with George. She walked on silently, hoping he would jerk and bounce on ahead of her.

But instead he kept talking. He leaped from subject to subject, from how he was teaching himself chess from a library book, to how next year he was going to join scouts, to what was her favourite colour. Peggy answered briefly and was relieved when they reached her gate.

"I'll just go home now, *next door*," said George.

"Okay. See you," Peggy answered.

She wondered which was worse — having no friends or being friends with a weirdo grade five next-door neighbour.

6

PEGGY went in the kitchen door and helped herself to a glass of milk and a handful of peanut butter cookies. She heard a crash from the living room. She put her head around the door and there was Dad, sitting on the floor, surrounded by piles of books, leafing through one of them. He looked up, startled.

"Oh, thank goodness it's you. I was afraid it might be Dorrie. I don't want her to find me until I have these books put away. She'll make me put them in Dewey decimal order or something. And then I'll never find what I need. Say, did you know that in Tibet people stick out their tongues as a mark of respect? How's school, by the way?"

For one crazy moment Peggy wanted to tell Dad the truth, to blurt out all that had happened. She wanted to tell him how lonely she was, to ask him what to do, and most of all to beg him to move the family back to Cedargrove. But how could she? Then she would have to admit the lie. He wouldn't be angry. But he would know how just plain silly she had been. She felt a wash of embarrassment just imagining it. She would have to get through this one on her own.

She gulped. "Okay. They play Chinese Skip the same way as at Cedargrove." They just don't play it with me, she added silently.

"Ah, yes," said Dad. "Children's games as an example of folk culture. I have an interesting article on that somewhere." He began to rummage in a box of magazines.

A lone book left in a big box caught Peggy's eye. *Keys to Happiness*. "Can I borrow this?"

"Certainly. And, Peggy, if you see Dorrie, distract her, all right?"

Nebbie was sitting in the kitchen sink batting drips with his paw. Peggy took the book outside. She was deep into an article written by an eighty-year-old doctor who said that if he had life over again he would take more risks, such as eating ice cream on his cornflakes for breakfast, when she heard the sound of sprinkling water from next door. She stuck her head through the hedge. Sing was there, swinging a large watering can back and forth over the newly greening rows.

He caught sight of her. "How is that cat?"

Peggy wriggled through the hedge and sat down in the dirt. "He's fine. He's sitting in the sink letting water drip on his head. That's what he always used to do at home, I mean in our home before, so I guess he's feeling okay."

"He likes water?"

"No. He hates it. Once we had to give him a flea bath and he nearly took Colin's finger off. But he seems to like torturing himself by sitting in the sink."

Sing moved over a row. Peggy shimmied over to keep up with him. "What's this row going to be?"

"Chard."

"Yuck."

Sing looked a question at her.

"It's horrible. It sits on the plate all soggy and oozes green water."

"But no. Just cook it a few minutes, until the leaves..." — Sing made a graceful opening motion with his hand — "... relax."

"Are you a cook? I thought you were a gardener."

"Cook and gardener both."

"Oh. I don't think I'd like relaxed chard any better than soggy chard."

Sing smiled. Peggy leaned back and watched him move up and down the rows, the spray from the watering can swinging in rhythmical arcs, leaving neat paths of dark brown. She felt a great easiness descend on her. Sing was a very restful person to be with. He was friendly but totally without that melty look that most friendly grownups got on their faces. And he didn't expect you to say anything. He was working, after all. Peggy opened her book and started to read "Ten Ways to a More Fulfilling Marriage."

Sing crouched down near her and began pulling grass from around the edge of a scalloped flower bed. "Leg better?"

"Yes. I went to school today."

"You like school?"

"No!"

Sing looked up surprised.

"Oh, I like my teacher okay, and the work. But all the kids hate me."

"Why?"

"Because I told this lie. I said that I used to have a horse but I didn't. And they found out. And now they hate me."

"Sounds lonely," said Sing. "Too bad." He weeded up a row and down a row and Peggy lay back on the grass, looking up through the leaves to the shining sky and letting the scenes of the lie and the arithmetic test and the lunchroom run past her mind's eye again.

"I had a horse once," said Sing as he came close again.

"You did?" said Peggy, sitting straight up.

"Yes, when I first came to Canada. In Victoria. My first job, a long time ago. I bought a horse and old cart from a coalman. And I walked around all the streets selling vegetables at houses. The horse was big. His back was this high." Sing patted his shoulder.

"What colour was he?"

45

"Brown. But mostly muddy. He got very dirty. Every day I washed off mud from the streets. But he was smart. Knew every house to stop."

"Did you have him for long?"

"No, soon I moved to Vancouver for a better job in a shingle mill. So I sold him." Sing made a trip to the compost box and returned.

Peggy moved down a row. "Did you miss your horse?"

"Yes. He was a good friend."

Peggy sighed. "I miss Fox, and he wasn't even real."

Sing looked up from the weeds. "Why did you lie?"

"It just popped out. Everyone was looking at me, waiting for me to say something, and I knew that I must look really stupid standing there. I didn't mean to say it but I did. I guess it sounds crazy."

"Not so crazy," said Sing. "I know that feeling. One day when I was a small boy in China I walked down the road near my village. I looked down dreaming and then I looked up and my cousins were walking along the road toward me. They carried a water bucket on a pole between them. They were talking to each other. All of a sudden I knew that I couldn't think of anything to say to them. So I jumped right into the ditch beside the road."

"And then what happened?"

"They came by and saw me and said, 'Why are you lying in the ditch?'"

"What did you say?"

"I said, 'Oh, no reason,' and then they went away." Sing paused. "I liked my cousins too."

"Oh, I know," said Peggy. "It doesn't matter if you like the person or not. We don't have ditches but sometimes I hide in the alley if I see somebody I know coming down the street."

Sing nodded and went quietly back to pulling grass. Peggy let the full surprise of his story hit her. She felt she had just met the first person in her life who spoke the same language. She imagined a little boy lying in a ditch. She knew he would try to sound very off-hand when he said, "No reason," and how he would peek over the edge of the ditch at his cousins as they walked away, wondering if they were laughing at him but wanting to be with them all the same.

"Hey, Sing. Do you, like, really hate it if people look at you?"

"Yes. It makes me go... frozen."

"Yes. Frozen. That's exactly it."

"Peg-gy." Mum's voice floated across the yard. "Dinner!" Peggy grabbed her *Keys to Happiness*. "Got to go. Bye, Sing."

7

THE next day and every day until the end of term Peggy spent after school in the next-door garden, visiting with Sing. She helped weed and stake tomatoes. Gardening, which had always seemed like a combination of boredom and hard work, started to be fun as she kept track of the progress of the carrots and the scarlet runner beans. Sing spoke of vegetables with the same pleasure that other people talked about flowers, and his enthusiasm was contagious. Best of all, he remembered more stories about the Lane family, and every day brought another chapter in "The Adventure of Daphne the Bad."

The new house was still a chaos of half-unpacked boxes. Mum dashed from mopping out cupboards to attending an endless string of welcoming teas. She said, "Invite anyone you like home after school," but she seemed to accept "Going out to play" as a good enough explanation of what Peggy was up to.

But two and a half weeks of school remained, two and a half weeks to just get through. Each evening Peggy tore off one page of her "Word for the Day" calendar and ripped it into tiny pieces. Wednesday — "truculent," *rip*, twelve days to go. Thursday — "vitreous," *rip*, eleven days to go...

When she was the last to be picked for sides in the softball game; when groups of girls fell silent as she passed; when Linda turned around in her seat and whispered, "So. Going to visit your *horse* this summer, huh,'' Peggy thought often of Sing and the ditch. But there weren't any ditches handy.

Mrs. Bristow made her blackboard monitor for three days in a row, letting her go out to the empty schoolyard during class to bash chalk dust out of the blackboard brushes. Peggy started to worry that the teacher had noticed something was wrong and was being extra-nice. So she made an effort to look happy and part of the gang. Then the year-end flurry of textbook counts and report cards left everyone too busy to notice much of anything.

She used lunch hours and recess to do her homework in the school library. There wasn't enough work to fill the time even when she was very careful. On her map of Africa she named all the countries and their capitals, printing against her ruler to keep the letters absolutely straight. Then she drew decorations of tiny animals and a perfectly shaded edge of blue around the coastline. She sat in the library rolling the names of the countries silently around in her mouth and revived her half-forgotten ambition to be a missionary. Surely in Basutoland and the Belgian Congo and Madagascar, among the hippos and cheetahs and hartebeests, it would be easy to make a fresh start. The next day Mrs. Bristow was so impressed with the map that she pinned it to the ''Homework of the Week'' bulletin board. That gave Linda the opportunity to add ''teacher's pet'' to her stockpile of insults.

Sometimes when there was no homework left, Peggy just sat at a table near the window and stared out, hiding behind a large book propped on the table in front of her. She pretended she was looking through Colin's microscope and observed how groups of kids formed and broke apart and re-formed, like little creatures in swamp water. She noticed how Linda was almost never alone and how George almost always was, doing solitary flips over the fence, sprinting around the edge of the field or staring intently at a bug on his finger.

The other boys, especially the gang around a skinny mean kid with curly black hair, teased George. But George didn't seem to notice. Sometimes Peggy wondered whether he was a slow learner, except that he did very well in school and even taught himself chess.

Peggy knew all about this because George persisted in walking her home. After school Peggy would pack her books very carefully into her bookbag in order to give the other kids time to leave. Then she would begin trudging up the hill, the load lightening as each step took her farther from school and closer to home, Sing and the garden.

But then she would hear George's cheerful "Hey, Peggy, wait up!" and there he would be, bouncing along, briefcase swinging, talking non-stop in his strange old-fashioned way.

One day, after he had described himself as "exceedingly hungry," Peggy got fed up.

"Why do you say 'exceedingly'? Just say 'very' or 'really' like everybody else."

"Is 'exceedingly' incorrect?"

"It's not wrong. It's just, you know, weird. Where do you get these words from, anyway?"

"From books." George bounced up onto his toes in enthusiasm. "I read aloud to my parents. We all improve our English together. My father said that Charles Dickens was a famous English writer. So I'm reading a book called *David Copperfield*. But if 'exceedingly' is not proper, you just tell me."

Peggy thought of Dad's collection of Dickens. She had poked in them once, but they had always looked too hard. "How long have you been in Canada, anyway?" she asked.

"Two years and three months," said George.

Peggy's irritation dissolved into grudging admiration. *Next-Door Neighbours* to Dickens in two years. Pretty good.

George *was* embarrassing, especially walking her home. But his voice was better to listen to than the one in her own head that kept reminding her how dumb she had been.

"Come on," she said. "Forget it. 'Exceedingly' is an okay word."

One day after school, when Peggy had been delayed by the music teacher who wanted to know whether she would like to join the band next year, she came out to find George surrounded by a gang of boys led by the skinny black-haired kid. They had stolen George's cap, a grey cap with ear flaps, and thrown it up onto the roof of the gym. George refused to climb up and get it. He and the skinny kid stood nose to nose.

"So what are you? A chicken?"

"Why do you call me a chicken?"

"You're scared to climb up on the roof, aren't you?"

"Do you mean that I'm a coward?"

"Yeah. That's exactly what I mean, Georgie-Porgie."

The gang made supportive noises in the background and one boy called out, "You tell him, Brian."

"But chickens aren't cowards. We had chickens on our farm in the old country. What chickens are is silly, not scared. They can even be quite brave in a stupid sort of way." And George stood earnestly looking at Brian.

This drove Brian crazy. "Yeah, well, you said it. Silly, stupid, and a chicken-liver."

"Good one," mumbled one of the gang.

Then Brian spat on the ground. "Come on, guys." They moved off.

George looked up at the gym roof and sighed. His face brightened when he saw Peggy. "Hi, Peggy. Isn't it funny how 'liver' is this thing — he pointed to the fifth button of his shirt — and something that lives?"

Peggy shook her head. "George, what are you going to do about your hat?"

"I guess tomorrow I'll ask the janitor to get the ladder and fetch it for me."

"George, I think you should forget it."

"Why? It's a splendid hat."

"But nobody else wears a cap like that, especially not in nearly summer."

"They probably don't have one like mine."

Peggy sighed. "It's just like that briefcase. Nobody else carries a briefcase. Don't you want to fit in?"

"But I don't see why my hat is important."

Peggy gave up. "Okay. Forget it. They've gone now. Why don't you just climb up and get your hat back and then you can go home."

George looked astonished. "But I don't want to climb up there. I hate heights."

"Then you really are a chicken?"

"Of course," said George happily. "I'm probably a chicken-liver even, if I knew what it meant."

Peggy grinned. George. There he was as goofy and hopeless and weird as ever but — she searched for the word — honest. She realized that what bugged Brian and the gang was not briefcases or caps, but that George always told the truth.

Since her big lie, Peggy had thought a lot about truth. In Sunday school stories people who always told the truth had a shining and horrible goodness about them. But George wasn't like that. It was as though it just never occurred to him to lie or have secrets or slide out from under a question.

She stared at George and thought about him as a friend. Suddenly having no other friends filled Peggy with a bouncing sense of freedom. She grabbed George's briefcase and spun around with it. "Hey, chicken-liver, do you want to come over to my place?"

Peggy opened the front door just in time to see Colin crashing in a jump from the first stair landing.

"Look at me!" he held his arms up like a prize-fighter. "I'm a tycoon! I've got a job for the summer and I'm going to be *rich!* Hang around with me, kid, and I'll make you a star! Hi, George." Then he explained that he had found a job in a pickle factory for July and August. "No more French verbs, no more causes of World War I, no more Shakespeare. Just pickles and money. Here, kid, have an ice cream on me. You too, George." And he reached into his pocket, handed Peggy a dollar and loped off into the kitchen.

"Gosh, a whole dollar. He *is* feeling rich. Come on, George, let's go to the store before he comes to his senses. We can cut through Mrs. Manning's yard. It's quickest."

Sing was in the garden and Peggy stopped to introduce George. "We're going to the store. Colin got a job in a pickle factory so he's treating us to ice cream. I think I'm going to have a double scoop neapolitan. George?"

"Soft ice cream for me."

"*Soft!* Boring. It only comes in vanilla. What do you like, Sing, hard or soft?"

"I've never had an ice cream cone."

"Never? Not once? That's terrible." Peggy fingered the dollar bill in her pocket and felt like a big spender. "We'll get you one. What kind would you like?"

Sing shrugged and grinned. "You decide."

At the store they bought the cones—double-cone soft for George, two-scoop neapolitan for Peggy, and vanilla but hard for Sing as a compromise. They ran back across the alley and in Mrs. Manning's gate as fast as they could, watching for any sign of drips.

"Okay," said Peggy, presenting Sing with his cone. "Here's what's best about hard ice cream. First of all you can bite it." She sank her teeth into the ice cream and felt the cold travel up into her skull, leaving a little buzzing ache on the top of her head.

"Here's what's better about soft," countered George. "You can shape it." He made his mouth into a little "O" over the ice cream and twirled the cone, recreating the pyramid with its curling point. "Besides, in soft the ice cream goes right down into the cone."

"Ah-*ha!*" said Peggy. "But if you're an expert you can do that with hard ice cream too. You just have to push it down as you eat. Like this." She demonstrated, finishing up each lick with a push from the top of her tongue. "Do you like your cone, Sing?"

Sing interrupted his careful licking. "Yes. And I like the lessons. A school for eating ice cream."

"Okay. Here's lesson two," said George. "But only for soft. It's good for moustaches." He pushed the ice cream against his lips and left a sticky white ring around his mouth.

Sing watched very earnestly and then, without a smile, he said, "Not just for soft" and copied George, smearing his own mouth with his fast-melting ice cream. After a second's shocked silence Peggy and George began to giggle. Sing gave a dignified nod and started to methodically lick around his mouth. His eyes were twinkling.

Peggy was in the middle of demonstrating her best trick, holding the cone above her head, biting off the pointed end and slurping out the remaining ice cream, when Mrs. Manning's bell rang.

"Oh," said Sing, and for the first time Peggy heard an edge of impatience to his voice and saw a flicker of annoyance pass over his face. But then he popped the rest of his cone into his mouth. He took a large white handkerchief from his pocket and carefully wiped his face. "Thank you for the ice cream and ice cream school," he said, and turned to walk toward the house.

8

"VOCIFEROUS." "Baffy." "Gallivant." One by one Peggy tore up the days and threw them in the garbage can. And then it was the last day of school.

She walked home with George as usual. His briefcase was bulging, and he was carrying a big piece of plywood with cut-up bits of plastic skipping rope glued on it — his project on the sewer system. Peggy had little besides her report card and a few notebooks. She felt relief that the year was over. No more staring at Linda's angry back. No more filling in time by copying her homework twice. But she also felt flat, with none of the break-out craziness that the last day usually held.

There would be no family holiday this year, with Dad just arriving at a new church. And Dorrie had a job like Colin. Mum had suggested summer camp to Peggy. Dorrie had been a keen camper, arriving home every year with braided plastic keychains, copper foil plaques and stories of overnight canoe trips. But it sounded like the rack to Peggy. Groups of strangers, every minute organized, no place to be alone. All the same she wondered how she was going to fill the long summer days ahead.

She didn't have to wonder long. The next morning George arrived at the back door waving a notice. "Hey, Peg! Look at this! I got it at the playground. Want to do it?"

Peggy took the notice and sat down on the back step.

Puppet Show Competition. Armstrong Park Playground Association announces a summer puppet show competition. Open to children aged eight to fourteen in teams of two. Performances will take place Saturday August 22nd. Shows limited to twenty minutes in length. Prizes donated by Quality Cycle: A pair of CCM Sidewalk Emperor Bicycles complete with baskets, kickstands, and deluxe decorated handlegrips. In choice of style and colour. Register before July 7th.

"See the prizes?" said George in an awed tone.

"But I've already got a bicycle," said Peggy. "Well, sort of, anyway. It's Dorrie's old one. She doesn't use it anymore."

"You have a bicycle and you don't ride it?" George asked incredulously.

"Haven't got around to it yet. And, well, I haven't ever ridden in the city and the bike is kind of big for me and I'm a bit scared."

"But look — 'choice of style and colour.' You could have one that is the perfect size. Don't you want to? It would be fun."

"Perform in front of an audience?"

"But you get to hide behind the stage. Come on. You'd be good." George was bouncing up and down in excitement.

Peggy thought for a moment. She did enjoy charades. She could talk in funny voices. And it was something to do for the summer. Better than just a long string of days. "Okay, sure."

They went to the park and signed up and then hurried home, discussing story ideas. "How about 'The Twelve Dancing Princesses?' " said Peggy. "We could have beautiful costumes."

"Twelve?" said George. "You would have to be an octopus. And I'd have to be half an octopus. We could do 'Tom Sawyer.' "

"Too long. I've got a dog puppet somewhere. Maybe we could do a dog story."

Mum met them at the door. "You haven't forgotten about lunch, have you?" Peggy had. "Miss Blatherwick from the altar guild is coming and I could use a hand. I'd also like it if you would change into a dress."

"Aw, Mum. George and I... we've got this project."

"You and George have the whole summer ahead of you. For the moment your project is lunch."

"Okay," said George. "I've got chores anyway. See you later."

Lunch took forever. Miss Blatherwick was the slowest eater in the history of the world. It was torture to watch her. She ate English style, like Dad, using her knife to load food onto the back of her fork. Bite by tiny bite she composed miniature abstract works of art on her fork. Tiny smear of potato salad, small perfect square of chicken, three peas. And then she would pause with her fork in mid-air as she talked. Peggy stared hard at the food, *willing* Miss Blatherwick to put it into her mouth. But, no. She was deep into a discussion of dahlias.

Finally, like the erosion of the Rocky Mountains, Miss Blatherwick's clean plate emerged.

Dessert crawled by, and when the last spoonful of fruit salad had made its tedious way into Miss Blatherwick's mouth, Peggy suddenly remembered that she had agreed to do the dishes.

She washed as fast as she could, sending soap bubbles flying up into the air. When she had finished, she dropkicked the wet dishcloth across the kitchen in celebration. It made such a satisfying splat on the wall that she did it again.

Now for the puppet script. She needed paper.

She went into the living room and tried to interrupt. It was tricky. Miss Blatherwick talked slowly but seamlessly. Peggy leapt into the first break. "Dad, can I have some paper?"

Most of the time Dad said, "Help yourself," but this time he went with Peggy down the hall to his study. He fished some lemon-yellow paper out of his desk. "I just got my latest joke sheet. Want it?" Dad received a magazine called "Notes, Quotes and Anecdotes," which was full of funny stories and jokes. It was for ministers and business-men who wanted funny bits to put in their sermons and speeches. Dad didn't use it because the funny bits he used were more likely to be funny-peculiar than funny-ha-ha. So he passed the magazine on to Peggy who loved to read it in the bath.

"Dad. Aren't you supposed to be visiting with Miss Blatherwick?"

Dad grinned. "Yes, but to tell you the truth I was getting a bit tired of dahlias. I think I'm going to have to go and make noises about having to compose a sermon or something."

Peggy escaped and found George, and they continued their discussion about stories. George had set his heart on Franklin's search for the Northwest Passage. He had taken to Canadian history in a big way.

"Think of it. Trudging through the snow to certain death." George made arctic wind noises through his teeth. "We could use cotton batting."

"But, George, puppets don't *trudge* very well. They're better at chase scenes. And I don't think that all the char-acters freezing to death is a very good ending. But I'm reading this great mystery story. It's got a cave and the kids become detectives. That would make a good show."

George said they should give it a try. But after a few pages they admitted the obvious — that writing, like read-ing, is better done alone. "You try it first, Peggy. I was supposed to finish helping Papa in the garden. Come and find me when you're done."

Peggy began by setting up her desk with a pile of paper and three needle-sharp HB pencils. She wrote furiously for three pages.

Dick: I think I see something shining up there on the rocks.

Sharon: Perhaps it is the treasure.

Harriet: But how can we climb up there? The cliff is so steep.

How *could* they climb up there? Hand puppets didn't have legs. Peggy tossed page three into the waste basket and took a fresh sheet.

Curtain. Scene Four. On the cliffs.

But that wouldn't work. You couldn't do a backdrop change after just one thing happened. Maybe it would be better if they found the treasure on the bottom of the sea.

Peggy chewed the end of her pencil. Then Sharon and Harriet could stay in the boat and Dick could just dive down by disappearing behind the stage. Then they could pull up the treasure on a rope. Would Dick have to look wet when he came up? Could you dip a puppet in water?

Peggy wondered whether beauty improvement might not be a better summer project than puppetry. She went into the bathroom and rubbed zinc ointment onto her rough knees. Start again.

Look! Here comes the man with the black beard. We had better hide!

But with three puppets hiding, would there be any room left for the villain? Peggy broke open the poppit beads she was wearing and sucked one end. A thick suffocating blanket of boredom settled on her. Why would anyone bother to listen to this? She didn't even want to bother writing it out.

She went to the bathroom again and cut her toenails. How did you know when you just had to keep on working and when to admit that it was a mistake? She went to find George.

He and his dad were both on their knees in the flowerbed, weeding.

Mr. Slobodkin was a tall man with thick grey eyebrows that stood out like awnings over his eyes, and deep lines down the middle of his cheeks. He stood up, brushed the dirt off his knees and shook Peggy's hand.

"Good afternoon, Peggy. George says you are being a writer."

He pronounced "George" with hard "g's" and three rich syllables. "Gay-or-gay." Peggy tasted the name in her mouth. She sighed.

"I don't think I am a writer. Writing a play is too hard." She plunked down and started pulling up tufts of grass and throwing them in the air.

"What's your story?" asked Mr. Slobodkin.

Peggy told him about the villain and the money he had stolen and hidden in an underwater cave, and the plucky children who succeeded where the police had failed.

"I think that story is too big," said Mr. Slobodkin. "You need a small story. Just a few people. And then things happen like this and this. Like your..." He pointed at Peggy's poppit beads.

Peggy crossed her eyes to look down. "I don't get it. What kind of things?"

"Like an old story. 'Once long ago.' That kind of story. George used to like one about a fox and a hare."

George looked up. "Is that the one about the bark house and the ice house?"

60

"I don't know that one," said Peggy. "How does it go?"

"I've never told it in English," said Mr. Slobodkin. "I'll try. Once there was a fox and a hare and they built houses for the winter. The fox built his from ice and the hare used bark. Then came bright spring. The ice house melted but the bark house stayed as before. So the fox went to the hare's house and begged to come in. But when he was inside, he drove the hare away and took the house for himself."

"The hare went along the road crying and met some dogs. The dogs asked him what was the trouble and the hare told them. 'Do not cry, little hare,' said the dogs. 'We will drive out the fox.' And they went to the house and began to bark loudly. But the fox said, 'If I jump out, if I leap out...' " Mr. Slobodkin looked at George.

"The fur will fly," said George.

Mr. Slobodkin smiled and continued. "And the fox sounded so fierce that the dogs ran away. Again the hare went down the road crying and he met a bear..."

As the story rolled on in Mr. Slobodkin's rich, rumbling voice Peggy saw what he had meant about poppit beads. First the dogs, then a bear, then a bull were all frightened off by the fox. And then, finally, came the rooster.

" 'You cannot help me,' said the hare. 'Dogs tried. A bear tried. A bull tried. And they are bigger than you.' 'Just watch me,' said the rooster. And the rooster called out, 'Cock-a-doodle-doo, I have a sickle on my shoulder and I am looking for a fox to cut up into little pieces.' And the fox called up the chimney, 'Wait a minute. I am getting dressed.' And the rooster called again, but louder. 'Wait a minute,' said the fox, 'I am putting on my fur.' And when the rooster called a third time the fox ran out of the house and the rooster cut with his sickle and missed the fox by this much." Mr. Slobodkin held his fingers a smidgen apart. "And the rooster went to live with the hare in the bark house and they were both happy. That's a story for you and a crock of butter for me.''

Even before the end, Peggy knew that it was the story for them. She could see the puppets moving across the stage. She could feel how neat and tidy it all was, and how much fun. She thought how awful it would be if someone took over your house, if she came home one day and Linda had moved into her room and wouldn't let her in. She could hear Linda's intimidating voice getting her own way — ''You're not the boss of me.''

George must have been having similar thoughts. ''That fox sounds a lot like Brian. What do you think, Peggy?''

''I think it'll be perfect. Thanks, Mr. Slobodkin.''

''Yes, thanks, Papa.'' Mr. Slobodkin pulled George over to him and kissed him. Peggy was surprised. Dad kissed her but he never kissed Colin. But George didn't act like it was out of the ordinary.

They spent the afternoon talking over the script, trying to make each scene a bit different. George thought of making the rooster sound like a movie gangster. He talked out of the side of his mouth. '' 'Where's da fox what stole dis house? I'm gonna rub him out wit my sickle.' ''

'' 'I just have to dry these dishes,' '' answered Peggy in a panic-stricken fox voice. '' 'I'm just brushing my teeth.' No, hold it. 'I'm just brushing my tail. Be right with you.' ''

Peggy lowered her voice to a bear growl and George made loud rooster crowing sounds. And then they wrote it all down.

George went to Peggy's for dinner and over dessert they read the script aloud. Dorrie offered to type it and went into Dad's study. When it was finished it looked very official, with the fox's lines typed in red.

They sat in the kitchen while Colin and Dorrie took their turn at dishes.

''What kind of puppets should we use?'' asked Peggy.

"How about those ones on strings?" said George.

"No. They always get tangled."

"How about sticking eyes and noses into potatoes," said Colin.

"Get out of it, you double-acting baking powder," said Peggy.

"You could always throw in the odd carrot for variety."

"Ignore him," said Peggy. Then she remembered the maracas she had made in grade four. Strips of paste-soaked newspaper laid on the lightbulb in layers, then dried and painted.

"Papier-mache," said Dorrie. "Good idea. And bodies made out of material. I'll bet Mum would help you."

"The Fox and the Hare" was in production.

9

THE next morning Peggy's eyes flew wide open at seven o'clock. No school. The fat stifling pillow creature who had been sitting on her chest every schoolday morning, gluing her eyes shut and telling her to roll over and go back to sleep, had disappeared. Instead there was only Nebbie, who crawled into the warm place Peggy left as she jumped out of bed.

The house was quiet. She went downstairs and mixed up flour and water in a jug. Then she checked the bathrooms. There was only one empty toilet paper roll in the wastepaper basket. She needed at least two to start. She looked at the half-empty roll on the holder. Then she gave the end a firm pull. Unwound, the paper looked like more than it did on the roll. She piled it on the back of the toilet. She rooted around in the sewing room and found Mum's remnant bag. There was some very rabbity-looking grey tweed from a pair of Dad's pants and some rust-coloured corduroy for the fox. Then she went down to the basement to look for newspapers. She was looking in an old toy box for some Plasticine when she heard a strangled cry from the kitchen.

"Pthah, pthah, pooey."

She ran upstairs. Colin was standing over the sink, rinsing his mouth out with water and spitting. Beside him was a bowl of Raisin Bran covered in...

Peggy gulped.

"Um, Colin? Did you think that was milk?"

"Of course I thought it was milk. What else is white and liquid and sits in a jug on the kitchen counter?"

"Cripes. I'm sorry. I'm getting ready for papier-mache."

"Oh, that's okay." Colin put on a martyred look. "I just have to go and put in a hard day at the pickle factory on a diet of flour and water. But don't mind me."

By the time George arrived, Peggy had set up everything on a card table in the attic. Mum said they should go up there so they didn't have to tidy their mess between times. It was hot but they opened all the windows and the trap door to catch the breeze. Mum approved the remnant raid, found Plasticine and an old feather duster for rooster feathers, and didn't mention the toilet paper.

Softening the hard lumps of Plasticine was the usual bore. Peggy tried breathing on hers to warm it, but it only got damp and slimy. George stepped on his with bare feet.

"Just like stomping grapes," he said, "for Plasticine wine."

But finally the clay started to give under their fingers and they pushed in eye sockets with their thumbs and pulled out noses and ears. George made a very sharp-looking fox and Peggy a goofy, Bugs Bunny kind of rabbit.

The papier-mache was messy. And George was slow because he kept trying to make silly word combinations with his newspaper strips.

"Listen. 'Royals scrambling for under-sized crabs.' 'Miss Blueberry incarcerated.' 'Elvis Presley leaves four homeless.' "

"*George!* Hurry up. They get painted over anyway."

"I know, but here's the very best one. 'Cucumbers pose nude.' "

Soon all six puppets were lined up on the table, grey and white and blank-eyed.

"When do we do the next layer?" asked George.

"When we made maracas we waited until the next day, but let's do all the layers at once. That'll save time."

"Don't they have to dry in between?"

"No. No, they don't."

By noon the puppet heads were covered in six layers of newspaper. In a giddy moment they had also papier-mached the legs of the card table. They set the heads in the sunny window to dry.

"What do we do next?" asked George.

"When they're dry we cut them in half, take out the Plasticine, glue the halves back together again and then we can paint them."

Before bed that night Peggy went upstairs to check on the heads. In the twilight they looked like ancient stone statues. She thought of fairy tales where the wicked enchanter turns people and animals into stone. She could hardly wait to give them eyes and bodies. God must have had fun, she thought.

George was as eager to get onto the next step as Peggy, and he turned up at eight the next morning. Peggy had already gathered together the bread knife, the paring knife, Colin's bowie knife in its leather case and the big bone-handled knife from the drawer in the buffet. She had white glue and poster paint and brushes laid out on the card table.

The heads looked more ordinary, but still good, in the morning light. They felt cold but dry. "Side to side or across the nose?" asked George, bread knife in hand.

"I think across the nose for the rabbit. Otherwise you'll have to cut his ears in half."

But when George tried to cut the rabbit's head, it dented instead of slicing. "Come on. Let me." Peggy grabbed the carving knife. She tried a careful sawing motion, but the head just dented more.

"Hey," said George, "don't wreck it." Peggy ignored him. She impaled the head with the knife, levered a slice wide enough for her fingers and ripped the head in half. It was a mess. One ear broke off. She tried to remove the Plasticine, and the half-head collapsed completely into a wad of damp newspaper and glue.

George picked up the fox and poked it sadly. "How come they didn't dry? Maybe we should have left it for another day or put them in the oven or something."

Peggy twisted the comb on the rooster angrily. "They'll never dry properly. They're just a wreck."

George looked puzzled. "But *why* didn't they work?"

Peggy threw the rooster onto the floor. "I don't know. Okay, okay. Stop looking at me like that. Maybe we should have left them to dry between layers, but I didn't want to wait that long. It's too boring. And it *might* have worked."

George didn't answer.

"Well, it *might* have. Are you mad?"

"Yes."

Peggy felt as though she had run into a brick wall. Usually if you asked people if they were mad they said, "No, that's all right," and then you were off the hook.

"I'm sorry," she said in a not-very-sorry voice.

"I'm sorry too."

That wasn't what you were supposed to say when someone apologized. Suddenly George's truth-telling made Peggy very angry. Inside she let rip. She didn't know what he was so mad about. After all, she was doing it all for him. He was the one without a bike. Besides, it was her idea and her Plasticine and her house.

She just managed to keep that voice inside, but burst out with, "So? It's not like you had any great ideas."

George picked up the mangled rabbit. "No. I didn't."

Peggy jumped up and headed for the trap door. "So, why don't we just forget it. This whole puppet thing is

67

pretty stupid anyway.'' She clumped down the ladder, jumping the last half, landed with a crash and went into the bathroom.

She sat on the laundry hamper and rubbed her chin on her knees. Zinc ointment hadn't helped one bit. She took Colin's razor from the medicine cabinet and ran it lightly across the rough bits, but it just grabbed and hurt. She gave her index finger a good chew and then put her face up against the mirror and watched her eyes swim together. It was going to be one long boring summer without the puppet show. And without George. Colin rattled the bathroom door.

''Peg? Is that you in there? Are you going to be much longer?''

Peggy flushed the toilet, brushed past Colin and went upstairs. If the puppet show was off she might as well tidy the mess and fold up the card table. But when she got back to the attic, George was still there, digging Plasticine out of the rabbit's ears with a pencil.

''Are you still mad?'' This time she really wanted to know.

''No. But I wasn't mad because the papier-mache didn't work. I was mad because you knew that it might not work and you didn't tell me. We could have decided together. It's both our project, you know.''

The air lightened. Peggy looked down at George, his spiky no-colour hair, his stubby fingers gripped around the pencil, his funny little-man clothes.

She thought of Nancy, her best friend at Cedargrove. Why was she my best friend, she suddenly wondered. Because she fit the best friend hole. Because she liked the same things I did. I could always count on her to pick me for a partner. Her family was like my family and she used to phone me every Saturday morning. But George didn't fit at all. He was a puzzle piece from another puzzle.

68

"You're right. I should have told you." She looked at the mess on the table. "What should we do now?"

George looked her straight in the eye. "I think we should tear off the paper, redo the heads and start all over with the *first* layer."

But starting over again just didn't seem to work. The first day the Plasticine had been obedient, as though it wanted to become a rabbit or a dog. But now George's fox wouldn't go foxy, and Peggy's rabbit remained imprisoned in the blue-green lump.

"Want to just forget it for today?" asked George.

"Sure," said Peggy with relief.

Mum said they could have anything they wanted for lunch, so they fried slices of bologna until they curled up into little bowls and slathered them with yellow mustard. They made some changes to the script and then George went home.

Peggy went out into the backyard and sat on the swing. She twisted around until the twined ropes reached the top of her head and only the tip of one foot touched the ground. Then she let go and twirled around and around, extending her legs to slow down and then tucking them under the seat to accelerate. In the final blur she saw Sing come out onto the porch next door.

She squeezed through the hedge and gave him the latest news report, including the papier-mache disaster.

"I remember a puppet show when I was a little boy," said Sing. "Not puppets on your hand. Shadow-puppets. Some men came to our village. I was very small but I stayed up late and watched the show. The story was about a beautiful girl. She was really a snake. There was a dragon. I remember smoke in the light of the candles. And there was a clown with an umbrella who did tricks. And music."

"How did they make the puppets?"

"I think of stiff skin. Light shone through and they were many colours. They moved just like people move. An old man slow and crooked and a young princess so graceful."

"But how did they move if they were stiff?"

"Like this." Sing reached up and picked a couple of leaves off the peach tree. The leaves ripped as he tried to make holes in them. "This doesn't work."

"Hang on. I'll get some cardboard."

"And scissors," Sing called after her as she backed through the hedge.

"Cardboard, cardboard," Peggy muttered as she ran in the kitchen door. "Mu-um." She wheeled into the living room. "Do we have any cardboard?"

Mum was sitting reading. She didn't look up. "Dad's dresser. Top drawer. Shirt cardboard."

Peggy raced upstairs. An idea was nudging at the edge of her mind. Cut-outs would be a lot easier and faster than papier-mache. She thought of how surprised George would be if she gave him a shadow puppet fox.

Then she remembered his firm voice. "It's both our project, you know."

She detoured with cardboard and scissors via the church and stuck her head in the Slobodkin kitchen window. George was peeling potatoes, but a few words in Russian from his mother dismissed him, and they headed across Peggy's yard and back to Sing.

Sing looked at the cardboard for a while and then, with a sure hand, he cut out a dragon's head and four lozenge shapes with spikes. He dug the points of the scissors into the ends of the shapes and attached the pieces with bits of twig. "Come," he said and moved to the back of the garden behind the compost box where the sun shone onto the fence. He moved the cardboard shapes slowly up and down, and a dragon undulated across the wood.

Then the head fell off. "We need another thing for the holes," he said, "and a knife to cut patterns. A dragon needs eyes and scales. Then you move each part with sticks."

"Hey, Peggy," said George. "We could—"

"Sing!" Mrs. Manning's raspy voice cut through the garden as she appeared around the corner of the compost box. "Didn't you hear the bell?" She noticed Peggy and George. "Oh, Peggy, dear, how are you? And this is — ?"

"I'm George Slobodkin, pleased to meet you."

"Ah, yes, the caretaker's boy. Having a happy summer, are you?"

"Yes, thank you," said Peggy.

They all stood in silence for a moment. Peggy noticed that Mrs. Manning's lipstick didn't match her lips.

"Well, time to run along now. Sing has work to do." Mrs. Manning headed toward the house.

Sing began to follow her and then turned back, grinning. He was still holding the headless dragon. He handed it to Peggy.

"Later," he said.

10

OVER the next week Peggy and George threw out the newspaper strips and toilet paper rolls. They scrounged cardboard, scavenging in shirt drawers and desks, cutting up boxes and ripping the backs off their school notebooks. Dad saw them using scissor points to gouge holes and told them they could use the hole punch in the church office. And he arrived home one day with a box of metal brads they could use to attach the pieces. Dorrie lent them her goose-neck lamp and helped them figure out a way to use paper straws and pipe cleaners as rods for each piece. Mrs. Slobodkin cut out a square of old white sheet, and Mum stapled it to a picture frame. "Don't tell your father," she said, "but this frame used to contain an oil painting of a moose, the gift of a grateful parishioner. Dad hasn't noticed that it's gone."

But Sing was the greatest help. Peggy got discouraged when her method of drawing a rabbit — blob body, blob tail, blob head and pointed ears, didn't work for a rabbit in profile. But Sing just thought for a moment and then made three or four quick sketches, the rabbit hopping alive at the end of his pencil. George had an idea for a really beautiful rooster with every feather outlined. But after half an hour with an Exacto knife he ended up with a pile of confetti. Sing suggested concentrating on an elaborate tail.

Sometimes Sing made notes in Chinese writing. Peggy and George begged him to teach them the secret of the tiny,

72

complicated characters, like a secret code. But they couldn't get beyond the simplest characters, for "sun" and "moon."

"Chinese *children* do this?" asked Peggy incredulously, remembering her own painful struggles to learn longhand.

"Yes," said Sing, "but it takes many years."

One day they were in the back of the garden with Sing trying to figure out how to make the ice house melt. The animal characters were propped up against the fence.

George had just finished demonstrating how the melting should look, and was lying, spread out on the ground, impersonating a puddle of water. Sing and Peggy were in the final gasping stages of a giggle fit.

"What's going on here?" Mrs. Manning came around the corner of the compost box carrying an armful of flowers.

Sing picked up his rake. Peggy swallowed the last of her giggles. George jumped up.

"We're making shadow puppets," he said eagerly, picking up the fox. "We're going to put on this show at the playground. Do you want to see how they work?"

Mrs. Manning didn't even look at the puppets. "Not just at the moment, dear. I'm rather busy and so is Sing." She turned to go and called back over her shoulder. "Sing? I believe we have lunch to think about, don't we? Now run along home, you two. We wouldn't want to become a bother, would we?"

After Sing had left, Peggy and George sat with their backs against the fence.

"Why didn't she want to see the puppets?" said George.

"She's just mean," said Peggy, drumming her heels on the ground. "She pretends to be so nice, always trying to get me to come over and visit. And she gives me these awful candies that taste like perfume. And then she tries to sound so lah-di-dah." Peggy stuck her nose in the air. "Run along home, you two."

"I know," said George. "Imperious."

73

"What's imperious?"

"Do this. Do that. Like a queen."

"Exactly," said Peggy. She began to pack up the puppets. "Phooey on her anyway."

Three weeks later Dorrie went out to Cedargrove for the weekend to visit friends, and she arrived home with two flats of strawberries. "Jam time," said Mum, and the next morning she started.

She was on her second batch and Peggy was sitting at the kitchen table reading comics when the doorbell rang.

"Stir," said Mum, handing Peggy the red-stained wooden spoon. Peggy heard a low duet from the front hall. "Oh, yes, of course, do come in. Not at all." The voices approached. "You won't mind coming into the kitchen, will you?"

The swinging door opened and there stood Mrs. Manning, dressed in a navy-blue silky dress and wearing a hat and white gloves. Behind her Mum was trying to tuck damp bits of hair under her headscarf. She hurried around the huge and immobile Mrs. Manning and snatched a dishtowel from a kitchen chair. "Please sit down. I'll just make a cup of tea. I'm afraid I can't really stop. I'm making jam, and you know what that's like."

Mrs. Manning gave a look that loudly declared that she certainly didn't know what that was like and sat down, setting her handbag gingerly among the jars on the table. Mum put on the kettle.

"You've met our youngest, Peggy, I believe."

Mrs. Manning nodded coldly. "Actually, Mrs. Davies, I was hoping that I might have a word with you in private."

"What? Oh, of course." Mum took over the stirring from Peggy. "Run along up to your room, dear." Peggy caught Mum's sympathetic glance and left the kitchen. She whizzed across the front hall, up the stairs, across the landing and quietly opened the back staircase door. Slowly, testing each step as she put her weight on it, she made her way down the stairs until she reached the door at the bottom. It was slightly ajar.

"... so all I was wondering is if you were aware how much time little Peggy was spending with Sing?" Mrs. Manning was saying.

"Well, they do seem to be good pals. I gather he's helping with a puppet show that Peggy and George are working on. I'm pleased that she's found friends and a project for the summer. It was hard for Peggy moving so close to the end of the school year. I think she's had a bit of a rough time making friends at school. And Gareth and I are so busy with the new parish."

Peggy felt her fingers go hollow with embarrassment. *Don't talk about me.* Especially not to *her.*

Mrs. Manning sputtered a bit. "Well, yes, of course. But Sing isn't exactly... I mean, don't you think she would be better off with companions her own age?"

"Interesting that you should say that. Hang on, I'll just turn this jam off."

Peggy could hear Mum switching into her tactful mode. The change was as clear as hearing a car change gears. With organists who played too loud, with altar flower ladies in a huff, with Dorrie when Dorrie was bossing everyone around — Mum pulled out her tact.

"... I've always been pleased for the children to have friends of all ages. So sad to be locked into your own age group, I've always thought."

Mrs. Manning gave an impatient sniff. "But Sing is supposed to be *working.*"

"Are the children interfering with his work?"

We're *not,* fumed Peggy. He goes right on working. Sometimes we help. He always goes away when that stupid little bell rings.

75

"Well, perhaps not exactly interfering but... can I speak frankly, Mrs. Davies?"

"Please do, Mrs. Manning."

"The thing we have to remember is that he *is* from another culture and they don't always see things as we do. And considering that he's a middle-aged man, I'm not sure that his friendship with Peggy is entirely... suitable. I mean, *why* is he cultivating this friendship?" Mrs. Manning was sounding a bit like Linda Hoskins, Peggy thought. Like a mean person with a secret.

"I got the impression that perhaps he was rather lonely," said Mum mildly.

"Humph," snorted Mrs. Manning. "At least I feel I've done my duty. I've spoken out. And now I'll be on my way, if you don't mind."

"But, Mrs. Manning, what is it that you'd like me to do?" said Mum in a voice more puzzled than tactful.

"Just have a little talk with Peggy. Woman to woman, as it were. And perhaps just a little reminder that Sing is paid to be working, not chatting."

The chair scraped on the floor as Mrs. Manning stood up. Mum offered her a second cup of tea and a jar of jam, but both were refused. Then they moved into the hall, and Mum ushered Mrs. Manning toward the front door.

Peggy sat on the bottom step for a while with her chin in her hands and strained to hear the murmured conversation in the hall. Mum came back into the kitchen.

"You might as well come out now."

Peggy opened the door. Mum was stirring the jam like mad. "And now it's all gone sugary. Wouldn't you know that she would come over when I'm in the middle of all this and not even wearing a girdle."

Peggy climbed up on the kitchen stool. "How did you know that I was there?"

"Believe it or not, I was twelve myself once. Did you hear all that?"

"Yup. But I didn't get it. What's she talking about? We *don't* keep Sing from working. That's crazy. And what's all that other stuff?"

"Crikey. I'm not sure either. What a tiresome old woman. Trying to talk to her is like trying to pin down a piece of jelly," Mum sighed. "Look, do you want a cup of tea? I could certainly use another."

"Okay. What's the matter with her, anyway?"

"I think that the real problem is that Mrs. Manning is an unhappy old woman who is living in the past. Millie Hoskins told me a bit about her. Seems her husband was some top-drawer lawyer and their family was really something. But now he's dead and she doesn't really have anybody. I imagine that she misses feeling important. Her family has always had a Chinese houseboy so she still has one, even in this day and age. But she doesn't really see Sing as a person, just as a servant. So when she sees you — and it matters to her that you are the daughter of the rector — spending time with him, I guess it undermines her authority somehow."

"But what was all that about woman to woman?"

Mum took a big swallow of tea. "I think she was implying, probably without even admitting it to herself, that your friendship with Sing is unhealthy, that he's one of those men who makes friends with girls just to touch them in ways they shouldn't."

Peggy felt like she was going to explode. "But that's... stupid! That's just not fair. She's lying." She jumped up from the table.

"Hang on, Peggy. I know that. But it's hard to argue with someone who is so... mealy-mouthed. Come back over here, pumpkin. Want to make wax fingers?" She handed Peggy a saucer of paraffin.

"Okay," Peggy agreed sulkily. She dipped her fingertips in the paraffin and let it dry. Then she carefully pulled off the little caps and set them along the counter. "What did you say to her in the hall?"

"I said I would mention it to you and that perhaps you would not go over there so often."

"That's not fair. We're just getting to the part of the puppet show where we really need him. To look at the show and tell us how to move the puppets better. You didn't even try to argue with her. I'm going to go over there whenever I feel like it." Peggy smashed each wax cap with her fist.

"But, Peggy, that's likely to make things that much harder on Sing."

"Oh. But how can she think that stuff and still live in the same house with Sing? That's so dumb."

Mum finished her cup of tea and poured another. "I suppose it won't hurt you to know this. Millie Hoskins told me. The thing is that Sing's room is in the basement. Mrs. Manning has a bolt on the door going down there from the kitchen. She locks it at night."

Peggy's anger dissolved, replaced by a sick emptiness. "We don't even lock Nebbie in the basement at night."

Mum reached over and hugged Peggy to her. Her voice was very quiet. "No. We don't."

11

A T dinner Dad had an idea. "If you're not allowed to go next door visiting, Peggy, why don't we invite Sing here? For a meal or something. What's his day off?"

"Saturday. He usually goes to Chinatown and visits friends."

"So how about next Saturday?"

"Sure," said Mum. "It'll be a busy day because of the rummage sale in the afternoon, so we'll make it a simple dinner, but that's okay. You're helping with the rummage, aren't you, Peggy?"

"Yes. George and I get to run a stall all by ourselves."

"Fine. I'll leave it to you to find out if Sing is free and to issue the invitation. Six o'clock. Invite George too. Then maybe you can work on your show after dinner."

"Great!" crowed Colin. "That'll really get old Manning's knickers in a twist."

"Getting Mrs. Manning's knickers in a twist isn't our primary motivation, Colin," said Dad, but his eyes were twinkling.

Sing accepted the dinner invitation with thanks. When Peggy told him about the rummage sale, he offered to come along in the afternoon and help. "Neat," said Peggy. "You can be on our stall. George and I get to be 'white elephant.' That's junk."

Early Saturday morning Peggy met Sing at the back of the church hall. As soon as they opened the door they were in

79

the thick of rummage preparations. Tables were set up along the edges of the room and in an island in the middle. People were scurrying around with armfuls of clothes, bundles of hangers and cookie tins for the cash. They called out to each other. "Has Jack turned up for housewares?" "Who stole the masking tape from men's shoes?" "Don't leave your hat there, Vinnie. We'll sell it." The air smelled of dust, mustiness and coffee.

Peggy and Sing spied George already on duty unpacking and arranging stuff on the white elephant table. They picked their way around the piled-up boxes and the rushing people and joined him.

A woman with dyed blonde hair, bright red lipstick and a cigarette in her mouth deposited three cups of thick milky tea on their table. "Have this. You'll need it to keep up your strength." She laughed like a seal barking. "I'm from next door." She pointed. "Ladies' shoes. Things to watch out for. First of all they'll steal you blind. Eyes peeled for open bags and big pockets. Second of all, they'll try to switch labels, so take a good look at your price beforehand and stick that masking tape down as hard as you can. Third of all, they'll try to bargain. Don't fall for it. The line is, 'The price is marked, madam,' or sir as the case may be. Got it?"

Peggy thought of the Christmas bring-and-buy sale in Cedargrove, a well-behaved event full of ladies in hats. "Do people really steal things from a *church* rummage sale?"

"Just wait," barked the shoe lady. "You'll see. Call if you have problems. On shoes I'm known as Sarge."

Peggy, George and Sing started obediently looking over their merchandise. A ceramic owl with a clock in his stomach; a bag of Scrabble tiles; a Brownie hawkeye land camera marked "as is" ("That means broken," said George); an inflatable rubber duck decoy; a nylon chin strap guaranteed to eliminate double chins; a barometer decorated with the signs of the zodiac; a big box of picture frames, some with pictures; a trumpet mouthpiece; a toy cash register; a Niagara Falls television lamp; a trivet that said "Kissin' don't last, Cookin' do''; and three boxes of stuff waiting to be put out.

George climbed onto a chair and looked out the high windows of the hall. "Hey, Peggy. Look at them all."

Peggy dragged over a chair to join him. She peered out. Winding away from the hall doors was a line of people stretching halfway down the block. "Wow! Are there always this many people?"

"Yup," said George. "It's a zoo."

At eleven o'clock the doors opened and a tidal wave of people poured in. The first hour passed in a flash. Peggy barely had time to look up from her cash box. Over the roar she heard the shoes sergeant barking orders and comments. "Good choice! The peek-a-boo pumps are very smart on you. Just the colour for fall." "No, I'm sorry, you *can't* buy just one shoe. The price is clearly marked, madam."

George put things in bags. Peggy made change. Sing caught people who didn't pay. At one point he dove under the table to collar a man who was holding a wheelbarrow-shaped ashtray and turning away into the crowd. "Cash desk is right here, sir, very nice ashtray."

Miss Blatherwick wandered by and spent twenty minutes holding viewmaster reels up to the light. "Now I wonder if my grand-nephew would like Rin-Tin-Tin or Wonders of the Deep. He's nine. How old are you, dear?" she inquired of George. Eventually she bought the whole set and wouldn't even take her change.

In the second hour the crowd thinned out a bit and Peggy was able to see the other tables. At ladies' dresses a large woman was trying on a dress by pulling it over her own clothes. "Harold! Get over here," came a muffled voice from inside the layers. "I need an opinion."

In the furniture corner Linda's dad, Mr. Hoskins, and Mr. Slobodkin were heaving a large bureau toward the stairs accompanied by a small woman in a big hat who fluttered beside them.

The shoes sergeant came over to visit. "I noticed you nabbing that guy with the ashtray," she said to Sing and punched him in the arm. "Good work. We need your type on shoes. I'll get you on my team next time." She glanced toward the door and grimaced. "Oh, no, here's Lady Muck. Trust her!"

Peggy was looking at Sing and saw the smile fade from his face and the curtains come down over his eyes. She turned to the door. There was Mrs. Manning standing in the doorway holding a cardboard garment box. Sarge sighed.

"Every year we put a notice in the parish bulletin saying that all rummage must be delivered the day before the sale, and every year Cora Manning turns up on the day with her one perfect thing to donate. Then she wants everyone to make a fuss of her. Lord love a duck!"

Sure enough, Mrs. Manning had made her way to the ladies' dresses table and was carefully opening her box while the ladies' dresses team hovered and the woman in two dresses struggled to free herself.

"There she goes," said Sarge, "probably trying to persuade them to charge some ridiculous price. At a rummage sale! Here you get a Dior for thirty-five cents!"

Peggy watched out of the corner of her eye as Mrs. Manning progressed around the room occasionally picking up something with her fingertips and holding it at arm's length. Then another wave of customers arrived at white elephant and took her attention. In the middle of assuring a teenage boy that the stag's head cuckoo clock was indeed ninety-eight cents and not eighty-six cents upside down, she heard Mrs. Manning's voice.

"And what do we have here? George, isn't it?"

A silence fell over the table.

"White elephant," said George, holding up a gold-painted macaroni wreath.

Mrs. Manning reached out her gloved hand. Sing, who had been pulling out a box from under the table, stood up.

"Good heavens!" Mrs. Manning's hand dropped to the table and her smile faded. "What are you doing here?"

"I'm helping," said Sing quietly.

"Well. Isn't that... nice." Mrs. Manning put on her smile again. "So, carry on. Such good work you're all doing."

Peggy watched Mrs. Manning as she walked down the aisle, past the housewares, around the bureau movers, and out the door. She had a sudden memory of walking out of the lunchroom at school, all by herself.

"Hey, Peggy," said George, holding up a tepee salt and pepper set, "are these ten cents for two?"

Dinner after the sale started out feeling a bit strange. Sing had suddenly turned into one of the grownups and not just Peggy's exclusive friend. But she did find out a lot about him that she hadn't known before. Dad jumped right in as usual and found out about Sing's life story, how he had come to Canada in 1922 and worked in a sawmill. How he had learned English in the mill and at the Presbyterian Church where they charged you ten cents for a snack and an English lesson.

"And a dose of scripture?" teased Dad.

"Yes, that too," said Sing.

Peggy's heart sank when the conversation turned to the closure of the sawmill in the Depression. As soon as adults started talking about the Depression, they always ended up by telling you how lucky you were.

Nobody mentioned Mrs. Manning.

After dinner Peggy and George ran through the show. Sing let them know when their hand shadows were getting in the way and when they were talking too fast. He noticed Peggy's recorder and suggested that they add some music. Then he helped them letter a poster to go on the front of the stage.

When it was time for Sing to go, Dad saw him out the front door and said all the host things. After the door shut Peggy ran upstairs and looked out the window, leaning her cheek on the cool sill. She saw Sing walk down the front path, turn in at Mrs. Manning's front gate, walk along the side of her house and let himself in the basement door.

"Pssst," she hissed. Sing looked up. "Good night."

He waved. "Good night, Peggy."

12

A FEW weeks later the playground posted the schedule for the puppet contest. There were seven entries. "The Fox and the Hare" was last.

"Phooey," said Peggy. "Now we have to be nervous all through the other shows."

Sing wasn't around when they got home, so they left a note on the hedge telling him what time the show was. Then, tired of everything about puppets, they went down to the beach for a swim.

Peggy swam her careful swimming-lesson crawl out to the raft, hooked her heels over its edge and floated on her back, daydreaming. George swam around and around the raft in a water-churning, goofy version of the sidestroke. On one of his swim-pasts, Peggy flipped over. "George! Come here. Where did you learn that stroke?"

George gallumphed through the water and grabbed the raft. "I made it up. I couldn't swim when I came to Canada, so I came down here and I watched everybody. Then I just taught myself. I like this way because you don't have to put your face in the water so much."

Peggy pulled her hair around her face to look like a mermaid. Typical. Just the sort of stroke that a cap-wearing, briefcase-carrying person like George would make up. Hope Brian never sees it, she thought.

After the swim George wanted to visit Quality Cycle and look at the bikes. But Peggy went on home alone. She thought if she saw her prize she wouldn't win it. When she arrived, Sing was in the garden. He waved her over.

"I can't come to the puppet show. I'm sorry. Mrs. Manning is having a tea on Saturday afternoon."

"But Saturday's your day off."

"Not this Saturday."

"Awww. Can't you come for just the show? It's only twenty minutes."

Sing shook his head.

Suddenly everything that Peggy liked about Sing — his patience, his evenness — just made her impatient. She kicked the toe of her runner into the dirt under the hedge and let her voice flatten out into a whine. "Don't you *want* to come?"

"I do, but it is not possible," said Sing quietly.

Peggy clicked her tongue on the roof of her mouth and turned away. "Yeah. Okay. See you."

She pushed through the hedge and flopped down on a deck chair.

"Peggy!" Dad called her from the church office window. "Can you come and give me a hand?"

In the office, piles of paper were arranged all around the edge of a large table, and Dad was standing in his shirt sleeves looking pink and bothered. "Miss Findley is off sick today and I've got to get this report out. It's taking forever and I have a funeral at three. Could you help? You just have to walk around like this, picking up the top sheet from each pile and then you staple it at the end."

"All right."

"You look very blue," commented Dad as they began circling the table in a strange, slow dance.

"Mrs. Manning won't let Sing come to the puppet show. She says she's having a tea or something." Thunk. Peggy punched the big office stapler with her fist.

"That's a disappointment," said Dad.

"Well, I think she's just being mean. It bugged her to see Sing at the rummage sale and now she's just..." Peggy thought of her word-for-the-day calendar "... retaliating."

"Yes. That's quite possible," said Dad.

Peggy stopped abruptly and Dad ran into her. "Can't you *do* something? She'd listen to *you*."

"I don't know, Pegeen. From what Mum says, Mrs. Manning's pretty hard to cope with. Let's just let things simmer down. It's too bad that Sing will miss the show, but he has seen it in rehearsal."

"But it's not the *same*."

Dad made two more circuits of the table. "Okay. Here's what I'll do. I'll drop over there this afternoon after the funeral and have a chat." Peggy tackled him around the waist in a big hug. "All right. All right. Back to work, you slave."

But later at dinner, Dad admitted failure. "She was sweet as pie and gave me a glass of sherry and everything, but she is adamant that she needs Sing on Saturday afternoon."

"Cranky old sump pump," said Colin. "She deserves one of those Old Testament punishments like a plague of frogs."

"Sometimes I wonder whether you quite got the point of Sunday school," said Mum.

Dad put his hand on Peggy's. "Sing can't come, but *I'm* free on Friday. Am I invited?"

Peggy brightened. "Sure! Sure you are. And, Dad?"

"Hm?"

"Thanks for trying with Mrs. Manning."

Dad slapped his hand to his heart and announced in dramatic tones, "For you I would beard the very lion in his den."

The morning of the puppet show, Peggy and George had one last rehearsal. Peggy forgot the opening lines and George sat on the mountain scenery and bent it so that it had to be recut, and it took ages to find more cardboard. They got mad at each other and made up and then transported all their stuff to the playground. Only five teams had turned up of the seven registered. Maybe other people had trouble with papier-mache too, thought Peggy. The audience was mainly puppeteers' families. There were lots of babies.

The three judges were introduced. There was a wrinkled skinny lady smoking a cigarette in a cigarette holder. She was from the Little Theatre Association. There was a teacher from the high school. And there was Mr. Malucci from Quality Cycle.

The first show was ''Punch and Judy.'' Peggy's heart sank. The puppets were beautiful, bright and sturdy, bought from the German toy store. But Punch mumbled and Judy used a monotone read-aloud voice. The scenes where they bashed each other on the head were a popular success, however.

By the time the second show was underway, a bunch of older kids had appeared. They hung around the back of the audience leaning on their bikes, pretending they weren't really watching.

''I hope Brian doesn't turn up,'' Peggy whispered to George. George just rolled his eyes.

Peggy tried to concentrate on the shows but she couldn't. She did a mental roll call of the puppets to assure herself that they hadn't forgotten any. But as soon as she ticked off the final one her mind flipped back to the top of the list again. She switched to worrying about what would happen if their lightbulb burnt out. She noticed that George kept sneaking peeks at his copy of the script. The sky clouded over and she pulled on a sweater.

Show number four was a one-puppet story about a girl and her garden. It was written as a poem. One puppeteer recited long speeches while the other made plastic flowers pop up above the stage. As the verses went on and on, the puppet dropped forward until she was lying like a dead thing in the middle of the flowers. Then a toddler ran up to the theatre and started to kick it. The toddler's mother just sat and smiled. The playground supervisor grabbed the toddler who began to bellow. The toddler's mother looked annoyed.

And then in the middle of the flower girl's last flowery speech, the sky darkened and giant splots of rain began to fall. Audience, puppets, judges, performers — all dashed for shelter under the overhang of the playground building. The rain fell heavier and heavier and began to hiss onto the grass. The toddler and the toddler's mother left.

All the adults began to make suggestions about what to do — delay until later, postpone until tomorrow, cancel. Finally Mr. Malucci poked his head into the equipment room of the playground building. ''Come on. Let's move in here.''

Everyone pitched in, collapsing the ping-pong table, moving the volleyball net outside, piling the mats at one end of the small room. The puppet theatre was wedged in the opposite corner and someone found an extension cord for the light.

Everybody crowded in and sat where they could. Peggy and George started to get organized. In the rush inside, the puppets and props had been gathered up every which way. Peggy lost her recorder and the Punch and Judy boy found it.

Peggy and George crawled in behind the puppet theatre, took the puppets out of the bag and began to tape up their script. George stepped on Peggy's hand, and a mosquito dive-bombed her left ear. She picked up her recorder and glanced at the line of music written at the top of page one.

''George! Look!'' she whispered. She pointed her recorder at the script. Without daylight the script was in darkness. The light for the puppets stopped at the bottom of the screen.

"Oh, boy." George tried to adjust the light, but it didn't work. The playground supervisor put her head around the corner of the theatre.

"Nearly set?"

"Er, yes, in a minute," George babbled. He turned to Peggy. "Is the sign out in front?"

"No, I forgot." Peggy scrambled around in the darkness and found the carefully lettered "Fox and Hare" sign. She stuck two hunks of tape to her fingers and squeezed out from behind the theatre. Her hands were trembling and she couldn't seem to breathe properly.

Then she glanced out into the audience. There was Sing, standing by the door. He caught her eye and smiled. And everything settled into place, like iron filings shifting into a pattern when a magnet is near. In the same glance Peggy noticed how happy the audience looked, pleased that they had not let the downpour wreck everything. Babies that had been crawling around on the grass sat quietly on their mothers' laps. The older kids had left their bikes outside and they lay on their stomachs on the piled-up mats. The room was quiet and dim except for the friendly hiss of rain on the roof and the light from the puppet stage.

Peggy attached the sign, announced, "Ladies and gentlemen, 'The Fox and the Hare,'" and ducked behind the theatre. She wiped her palms on her shorts and picked up her recorder.

"Come on, George. We don't need the script. We know if off by heart."

George gulped, nodded, picked up Fox, and they began. From the very beginning it felt like settling into a comfortable armchair. Without the script Peggy felt that she was really talking to George.

After a few minutes the audience began to boo whenever Fox appeared. It began to feel as though they were all making the show together. George said a few lines in Russian as Fox drove Hare out of the bark house. The bull's loud moo was such a big success that Peggy added several more. During the final music George began to whistle along, in a loud fancy syrupy way that made Peggy giggle into her recorder.

At the end, the applause echoed around the room. Dad shouted ''Bravo,'' and the kids on the mats stuck their fingers in their mouths and whistled. Peggy and George made the puppets bow and then it was time to come out from behind the theatre. They punched each other. ''You go first.'' ''No, *you* go first.'' But finally they were mobbed by the audience who wanted to see how the shadow puppets worked. The judges went outside to deliberate. Peggy left George to demonstrate and went to find Sing.

She slid her hand into his. ''You came after all! Did Mrs. Manning change her mind?''

''No, but the ladies are having tea and talking. I just came for a few minutes.''

Peggy bounced up and down. ''Did you like it?''

''It was very good. In this dark room the puppets looked better than outside. You could see every feather on the rooster's tail.''

The judges came back and everyone sat down where they were. The schoolteacher did most of the talking and said how much work everyone had put into their shows and how creative everyone was and how they had had a hard time deciding on a winner. And then he welcomed a photographer from the newspaper. Finally he looked at a piece of paper. ''And the winning show is... 'Fox and Hare' performed by...''

Everyone started to clap and hoot and the teacher gave up. Peggy and George went to stand in the doorway and started to shake the judges' hands. Suddenly George popped into the audience and found Sing. They stood on either side of him and took a bow. The photographer snapped a picture. Mr. Malucci presented them with their bicycle certificates.

Then everyone stepped out into the rain, through which a watery sun was making an effort. The photographer came and asked their names. "Margaret Jean Davies," Peggy told him.

"And who was that Chinese guy with you?" the photographer asked.

"His name is Sing Lee," said Peggy, "and he's..." She faltered.

"He's our puppet designer and our friend," said George.

13

THE picture appeared in the paper on Sunday morning. The front page was a collage of photos called "Summer in the City." There were shots of children building sandcastles, paddling on surfboards, selling lemonade and, right in the middle, bigger than the rest, was the picture of the puppet winners. George was squinting, Peggy's glasses had slipped down her nose, and between them was Sing staring straight into the camera, the beginning of a smile brightening his face. The caption said, "Winners of the Armstrong Park summer puppet show competition Margaret Jean Davies, 12, George Slobodkin, 11, with friend Sing Lee."

Mum sent Peggy to the corner store to buy eight papers so that she could send copies of the picture to all the prairie relatives. Then she remembered the English aunts and sent her out to buy three more. At the morning service lots of people turned up with clippings from their papers. By the afternoon they had thirty-seven copies of the picture, and even Mum was running out of relatives. "I wonder if Greatuncle Julius would like one. On second thought, I think he's dead."

Even with the distraction of the photo, Sunday was the longest day in the history of the universe. Peggy read over her gift certificate so often she had it memorized. She took the Eaton's catalogue over to George's place and they discussed every detail of every bicycle. They walked up to Quality Cycle to look through the windows. They went by the main street to see if anyone recognized them because they were famous. "We won't look snobby or anything," said Peggy. "We'll just look friendly and like we would be happy to sign autographs."

But even though they kept nice open friendly faces all the way down the street, nobody seemed to recognize them. And then their faces got tired.

Time had stretched out like pull taffy, and it was still only 2:30. Later Peggy hung around the backyard hoping to give Sing some copies of the picture. But he didn't appear all day. Colin took pity on Peggy after supper and played a few rounds of Parcheesi with her. And then, mercifully, it was bedtime.

Mr. Malucci wasn't surprised when they turned up at nine o'clock on the dot Monday morning. He had their bicycles assembled and ready. All he had to do was adjust the height of the seats. George's was maroon; Peggy's blue. They shook hands with Mr. Malucci, Mrs. Malucci and their grownup son Joe Malucci, and carefully wheeled their bikes out the front door of the shop.

Peggy ran her hands over the cold brightness of the fenders and spun the pedals. The red jewelled reflectors flashed in the sun. Even the tires were clean.

"Where should we go first?"

"A big field, I guess," said George, "so I can learn how to ride."

"George! Don't you know how to ride a bike?"

"Nope. I've never been on one."

Peggy remembered her weeks of training wheels and Dad carefully guiding her up and down the driveway. She swallowed a sigh of impatience. "Okay. Let's go down to the schoolgrounds."

When they arrived at the school she held George's bike as he climbed on. She expected to run beside him and hold him up. But no sooner was his leg over the bar than he gave a powerful push and sped off across the field, wobbly but upright.

"Steer!" yelled Peggy as George approached the chain-link fence. "Use your brakes!"

But George did neither. Instead he ran right into the fence and fell off, his bike landing on top of him. Peggy ran across the field.

"Are you all right?"

"More or less," said George, spitting on his handkerchief and wiping off his bike. "I guess I should have found out how to stop before I started." He picked some gravel out of his knee. "I'll try again."

After half an hour George was riding as though he had been born on a bicycle. They took a break and sat down against the fence to discuss where they should go and if they should take a packed lunch from home. The two bicycles, balanced delicately on their kickstands, looked as though they were having a conversation of their own.

Then across the deserted field came one lone bike-rider. Brian. He rode over the gravel very fast toward them. Peggy retreated behind the fence, but George stayed where he was. At the last minute, Brian wrenched his handlebars and skidded to a stop.

"So I guess you think you're pretty good, eh, with your picture in the paper?"

George didn't say anything. He just smiled.

"Pretty sick if you ask me, a guy playing with dolls."

George left a long pause. "Puppets. Not dolls."

Brian snorted. "Same diff. But that's not the sickest thing. You know what the sickest thing is?"

Again George left a long pause before saying in a low voice, "No."

Brian let his bike fall to the ground, stepped over it and moved very close to George. "You don't even know, do you? You don't even know what the sickest thing is?"

George did not move away. "No."

"First you hang around with girls, and then you hang around with some old Chinaman. That's the sickest thing."

Peggy's hands turned white as she gripped the fence. She felt dizzy. George took one step forward and a flicker of fear passed over Brian's face. They stared at each other for a moment.

Then Brian laughed and grabbed his bike. As he swung his leg over the bar, he yelled, "Chicken-liver."

George turned, walked the few steps to the school building and punched the brick wall with his hand. Then he turned to Peggy.

Peggy swallowed. "I guess Brian is pretty jealous, eh?"

George didn't smile. "I nearly hit him. I really wanted to hit him." He sat down with his back against the wall. "But I promised Papa that I wouldn't fight. I promised him that I would talk. But, Peggy," George clenched his fists, *"I lost my English.* In Russian I was screaming at him, but in English I couldn't say anything."

"Weird." Peggy noticed that George's hand was bleeding, and she handed him a tattered Kleenex.

They walked their bikes up the hill in silence. It was not the easy silence of two friends. It was the silence of Peggy thinking of things to say and then rejecting them as silly.

She dropped George at the church and carried on home. The sound of singing came from the open basement door. Mum was doing laundry. Peggy pushed her bike down the few steps. Mum turned, her arms covered in soap suds.

"So this is your prize. What a beauty. Did George get his too?"

Peggy burst into tears.

"Pumpkin, what's wrong?" Mum sat down with Peggy on a packing box.

Through sniffles Peggy told the story of Brian. "... and I *hate* him."

"Yes," said Mum thoughtfully. "Bullies. You usually find that someone is bullying them and they just pass it on."

"Oh, stop being so *understanding*," said Peggy, jumping off the box. "I don't *care* why Brian is a bully."

Mum smiled. "Oh, Peggy, of course you don't. Not at the moment. What a nasty incident though. Do you want to wring?"

Peggy nodded and picked up the long wooden spoon to lift hot soggy bits of washing out of the tub. She began to feed them through the wringer. She imagined feeding Brian's arm between the rollers. As his arm passed through, all the bones would crush and the blood would be pushed up to his shoulder. She shivered.

Mum dumped a new load into the tub. "The interesting thing about bullying is that sometimes there's a person who gets bullied and doesn't pass it on. Like George. Those are very brave people, and rare. I'm glad you've made friends with George, Peggy. Good picking."

Peggy remembered how she had avoided George when she had first met him.

"On the subject of friends, pumpkin, I've got bad news. This is probably an awful time to tell you, but... oh, these can soak. Let's go upstairs."

What bad news could she have, wondered Peggy. I've only got one friend and I know all about him.

Mum plunked down at the kitchen table. "I had another visit from Mrs. Manning this morning. She has fired Sing."

"What!"

"Apparently she didn't know that he had gone to the puppet show on Saturday until she saw his picture in the paper. He must have just slipped out for half an hour while she was entertaining her ladies to tea. Anyway, she was very upset and going on about how she couldn't trust him anymore, and so she let him go."

It's because I asked him to come, thought Peggy. It's because I whined.

"But that's stupid. Half an hour. It's not such a big deal."

"I know. I tried to reason with her. But, being Mrs. Manning, she doesn't say what's really going on. I have a feeling that she was just looking for an excuse to fire him. There's an independence about Sing that really gets her goat. I think she has a shock coming, though. He's not going to be easy to replace."

Peggy jumped up and headed for the back door. "I've got to see him before he goes."

"But that's the thing. He's already gone. And Mrs. M. is quite peeved about that too. Oh, she is a tiresome old thing. But I am sorry you didn't get a chance to say goodbye to Sing."

It *is* my fault, thought Peggy, remembering her impatience with Sing. I *wanted* him to disobey her. I *wanted* a show-down. If it wasn't for me he wouldn't have gotten fired. And I'll never get to see him again and say I'm sorry.

She opened the fridge and looked inside without seeing anything. Then she slammed it shut.

"Gotta find George," she announced and stomped out the kitchen door.

14

PEGGY found George in the church hall angrily throwing a tennis ball against the back wall. Throw, bounce, catch. Throw, bounce, catch. Throw, bounce — "Hey, George." The ball rolled away into a corner.

"Mrs. Manning fired Sing."

"What! Why?"

"Because he came to the puppet show. She didn't know he had come and then she saw the picture in the paper."

George got to the point right away. "It's our fault, isn't it? Okay, we've got to go over to Mrs. Manning's and tell her that it's our fault and make her unfire him."

"But he's gone."

"Gone where?"

"Nobody knows."

"Then we've got to find him. Maybe he's with some friends. Do you know the names of any of his friends?"

"No." I knew him in the garden and at our dinner table, thought Peggy, but I didn't know him anywhere else.

George retrieved his ball and bounced it hard on the floor. "We could bike down to Chinatown and look around. No, that's stupid. We'd never find him."

"Maybe we would if we had a clue," said Peggy. "He went in such a hurry. He probably left some stuff behind in his room. A letter or something. All we have to do is get into the basement and search."

"I don't know," said George. "It sounds as if we're trying to be the Hardy Boys or something."

Peggy intercepted the ball and pitched it across the room. "But we can't just do *nothing*. That's what everybody does. *Nothing*. Mrs. Manning tells lies about Sing and just gets away with it. Brian calls him names and what do we do? *Nothing*. Then he gets fired for no reason at all and now everybody's going to do nothing. I don't care if it seems corny. We've got to *try*."

"Yeah, you're right," said George. "Okay. Two things to find out. How are we going to get in, and when will Mrs. Manning be out of the house."

"I've got an idea for that," said Peggy. "She's in some ladies' group at the church. I'll ask Mum when the next meeting is. And I guess we just have to hope that she doesn't lock her basement door."

Peggy talked to her mum and discovered that the next meeting of the women's guild was in two days. She and George decided that the only way to find out about the door was to wait until Mrs. Manning went out and sneak over and try it. The next morning they took apples and lemonade and comics up to Peggy's room and sat where they could look down at Mrs. Manning's house. They took turns watching. At 11:10 when Peggy was on duty and George was deep in a Little Lulu comic, Mrs. Manning came out her front door carrying a shopping bag.

"Look, George, now's your chance. Don't go in or anything. Just check."

George wasn't much of a detective. Instead of sneaking around the bushes into Mrs. Manning's yard, he just walked through the gate, waving up at Peggy as he did so. Peggy tried to make "be sneaky" gestures, but George just looked confused so she gave up, and he disappeared around the corner of the house. He reappeared almost immediately, shaking his head and giving a thumbs-down sign.

"Try the kitchen door, then," Peggy whisper-yelled.

"What?" replied George.

"Shhhhhh." Peggy hooked her feet around the headboard of her bed and leaned as far out of the window as she could. "Kitchen door!"

"Oh, all right." George loped off again. This time he was away longer but came back grinning. "A-okay. Kitchen door's open. What time's this meeting tomorrow?"

"Two o'clock."

"I'll be here with a flashlight."

George arrived early, around one, and they settled in at the observation window with cookies to pass the time. But no sooner had Peggy broken open the package than Mrs. Manning walked out her front door.

"Yikes," said Peggy as she jumped up, scattering cookies everywhere. "She sure leaves early. This is it. Come on, George." She grabbed her knapsack and handed George his flashlight.

They crept out the back door and pushed through the hedge. After checking that all was clear, they slid quickly up the stairs onto Mrs. Manning's back porch, opened the kitchen door and stepped into her kitchen.

"Where's the basement?" whispered George.

"Must be over there," said Peggy, spying a door at the far end of the room. As she opened it, she ran her hand across the bolt and remembered what Mum had told her. "Come on."

As they pulled the door shut behind them, the basement seemed a pool of darkness. Peggy began to wonder if the break-in was such a good idea after all. But George flicked on the flashlight and pulled her by the arm.

They tiptoed down the worn wooden stairs. George circled the flashlight beam around them.

To their right were lines hung with washing, underwear mostly which, at a different time, would have been quite funny. Behind the clothes were two big concrete sinks and a wringer-washer. They ducked under the lines and Peggy jumped aside as something cold and hard — a garter? — brushed her cheek.

Beyond the washing the room was a bit brighter, as some determined light found its way through two grubby windows. A dusty workbench covered with jars and newspapers stood beside a swinging plywood door. George pushed open the door to reveal a toilet and sink. The sink was cracked and stained, and the toilet made Peggy think of stories about things swimming in toilet bowls. George let the door swing back.

"It doesn't look as though anyone lived here," he whispered. "Where is Sing's room?"

In the far corner were two doors, one full-sized and one starting halfway up the wall, like a cupboard. Peggy opened the bigger door. The flashlight beam flickered over jewel-coloured jars of preserves and pickles.

"Let's try this one," said George, struggling with the smaller door. But the bolt was stuck shut. Peggy grabbed a hammer from the workbench and bashed it. The bolt slid and George pushed the door open. "Hey, look at this!"

The opening led outside, to a latticed-in place under the front porch. It had a beaten floor and was filled with a soft greenish light as the sun made its way through the vine-covered lattice walls. It was like a room with living wall-paper. Peggy had her knee up on the sill when George pulled her down.

"Come *on*. We don't have time."

They pushed the door closed and it squeaked, making Peggy jump. She felt like a puppet that could be jerked out of control at any minute.

"Where *is* it?" she asked in a low voice.

George pointed at a dark corner between two pillars. "Must be there. It's the only place we haven't tried."

They felt their way around the big furnace. George bonked his head on a low-hanging pipe, and Peggy gave a nervous giggle.

"It's not funny," he complained. Behind the furnace was a curtained opening. George slid back the curtain, and there it was.

They looked into a small room with wallpapered walls, lit from a window covered in a flowered plastic curtain and a lightbulb hanging from the ceiling. There were two pieces of furniture — a narrow iron bed with sharp-looking corners, and a big carved dark-wood sideboard with cupboards and drawers and a long mirror built across the back. It took up about a third of the room. The floor was covered in linoleum, worn near the door. A chain was attached to the central hanging bulb and George pulled it, but nothing happened. He pushed back the plastic curtains and turned off the flashlight.

In the new light they could see the walls more clearly. What had seemed like wallpaper was really a collection of pictures. Pictures from magazines and calendars of waterfalls, weeping willows around ponds, English country gardens, rushing rivers, sunsets, snowy hills, autumn leaves. There were a few with animals and birds but none with people.

They stood looking, not saying a word, until Peggy felt her feet grow cold on the linoleum. They forgot about searching for clues. Peggy was kneeling on the bed to have a closer look at an African plain when they heard it. Footsteps above them.

"Crikey," she whispered, taking a look at her watch. "It's only been ten minutes."

"Don't panic," said George. "We can just go out the basement door. If she's above us she won't be looking out the back." Peggy grabbed her knapsack, George pulled the curtains back into place, and they started to slip around the furnace. But just at that moment they heard the door at the top of the stairs open.

Peggy quickly visualized the basement floorplan. The stairs showed a full view of their route out the door. She retreated, stepping right on George's toes. She tried to push him back into Sing's room. But George shook his head madly and pulled her around the furnace toward the high-up door in the wall. She could hear Mrs. Manning's heavy deliberate feet on the stairs. They scrambled up into the high door as quickly and quietly as they could, and George pushed it closed behind them. Then they sat trying to breathe quietly.

Peggy looked down and saw that she had grazed her leg in the climb and that tiny beads of blood were appearing. Soon it would start to hurt. She looked away.

George had his ear to the door. He made a gesture of opening a bottle. Mrs. Manning was going to the preserve cupboard. As soon as she went upstairs they could sneak out the basement door and escape. But just on the edge of feeling relieved, Peggy heard it, a tiny but definite sound. The sound of the bolt on the inside of their door being pushed into place.

George began to pull on the door but Peggy stopped him. "Wait till she goes." She waited while the sweep second hand on her watch made three endless rounds. Then she put her ear to the door and gave George the okay sign. He pulled hard on the metal handle. The door budged slightly and then stopped.

They looked at each other. Peggy felt giggles bubbling up in her throat. The grimmer George looked the more hilarious she found it. She swallowed her laughter for a minute.

"Well, now we're stuck. What should we do?"

George just shook his head, and Peggy had a moment's impatience at him being so unhelpful. They were in a spot, but the place was such a wonderful secret discovery that she didn't really mind. She looked around and found a pile of rusting gardening stuff at one end of the leafy room. "Look. We'll be okay. There's the end of a hoe here, and a garden fork. We can just dig our way out. You know, like dogs."

She handed the hoe to George. "I'll loosen up the dirt and you can dig it away." She set to work under the lattice wall.

But it was more difficult than it looked. The ground was baked hard. The few weeds that grew in it were like plants encased in concrete. She scraped away energetically. "Just pretend that we're prisoners, digging our way to freedom." Then her hands began to ache and burn. She became aware that George wasn't saying anything.

She looked over her shoulder at him. He was just sitting still, holding the hoe so hard that his knuckles were white. He had a dazed look in his eyes, and beads of sweat had broken out on his forehead.

"George? You don't need to be so worried. We'll get out. At the very worst we'll have to call somebody to come and rescue us. We'll get into trouble but not that much trouble. Are you sick?"

George pushed the words out of his mouth. "It's being locked in. It's that feeling of being trapped."

"But, look. You can see outside and everything." Peggy crouched down in front of the huddled George and tried to meet his eyes. But he just shook his head and made himself smaller and smaller.

The day suddenly lost all its sense of being a game. Peggy had to get George out, and quickly. She turned to her digging, but after a few more hot minutes she realized that it was no use. It would take hours to dig a tunnel.

She leaned her forehead against the lattice lathes and closed her eyes. The lattice bent slightly against her weight.

She took a closer look at how the wall was constructed. Each piece of lathe was nailed with one nail to a frame at each end. She grabbed the hoe out of George's hand and wedged it behind one of the lathes. As she pulled, the lathe separated from the frame with a slight squeak.

"It's all right, George. We'll be out in a minute." Peggy pulled on the boards that went one way and pushed on the boards that went the other until one corner was a hole big enough to crawl through. Then she grabbed George and half-pushed him out of the opening. He stumbled to the hedge, got through, and made it to the side of Peggy's house before he threw up into the bushes.

Peggy searched her pockets and found one bedraggled Kleenex. "I'll be right back." She returned next door and pushed the lathes back into place, pulling the bushes and vines up around them.

George was still sitting against the house looking pale and shaky, so Peggy went inside and fetched him a glass of water. He rinsed out his mouth. "Thanks."

"Hey, George? What happened to you in there?"

"It's being locked in. I can't stand it. It's because... when we were leaving the old country we spent some time locked in a train and we had to be very quiet and..." George's voice stopped in his throat and he leaned over again.

"Hey, it's all right now." Peggy's hand took on a life of its own and was making its way toward George's hair before she caught it. Her face grew hot. Sounding in her own ears like a Brown Owl, or some other sensible person who always knew what to do, she said, "Come on then. You need soda crackers. That's the only thing after you've thrown up."

Peggy was surprised to find Mum in the kitchen. "What happened to the women's guild meeting?"

"Oh, the president has catarrh so it was cancelled. What's the matter with you, George? You're white as a sheet."

106

Peggy rummaged in the cupboard. "He threw up. I'm going to get him some soda crackers."

"Poor you," said Mum. "Time for the medicinal ginger ale, I think." They all had some, in ice-tinkling glasses.

With her confusion about George, Peggy didn't give a thought to the purpose of their break-in until she lay in bed that night. A breeze was blowing in her wide open window, bringing with it the smell of sweet peas. It blew her curtains across her face. She reached up to touch them. They were yellow, with a small pattern of mauve flowers. Mum had made them for her last birthday. They matched her yellow chenille bedspread.

Beside her curtains, in her mind's eye, hung the plastic ones in Sing's room, the cold linoleum, the stained sink. She looked at her ornament shelf of lovely ceramic ladies, at her desk, her books, her framed paint-by-numbers, and she thought of people in small, mean places — Sing in his scene-decorated basement, and George in his railway car. The Peggy who had sneaked into Mrs. Manning's basement suddenly seemed like a child years younger than herself, a child she could barely remember being. She punched a hollow in her cool pillow and gave in to sleep.

15

P EGGY slept late the next morning, coasting in and out
of a dream in which she had to strip the wallpaper from
an endless wall using only her fingernails. As she fought to
the surface she heard a voice saying, "You can't just do
nothing."

She scrubbed her face and hands with Colin's gritty soap,
brushed her hair and parted it exactly, pulling it back into
a tight ponytail and sliding her new blue barrettes along
either side. She put on a skirt and blouse, white socks and
sandals. She headed down to the deserted kitchen where she
ate a banana that her stomach did not want. She heard the
sounds of a radio and of water running, but she did not try
to find anyone. Then she made her feet take her out the
front door toward Mrs. Manning's house.

Only at Mrs. Manning's gate did the panic start to rise.
But she kept walking, along the flower-lined path and up
Mrs. Manning's steps. On the front porch she ran her knuckles across the stucco wall until it hurt, took a deep breath
and rang the bell.

There was a long wait and Peggy, flooded with relief,
turned to go. But then the door opened and Mrs. Manning
stood there.

"Why, Peggy, hello. How nice that you've come for a
visit."

Peggy followed her down the dim hall toward the living
room. She stubbed her toe against a wrought-iron umbrella
stand as she blinked to get used to the darkness.

"Sit down here, dear."

Peggy perched on the hard couch in the living room. Mrs. Manning bustled about, pushing back heavy velvet drapes and raising roller blinds, letting the light in through lace curtains.

Peggy wiped her damp palms down her skirt and tried to think of what to say. She took a couple of breaths and opened her mouth.

"Floral gum?" asked Mrs. Manning, passing her a silver candy dish.

"No, thank you."

Mrs. Manning lowered herself heavily into a purple chair. "I'm afraid I can't offer you any other refreshments. Sing has left, just like that, and things are all at sixes and sevens. Such a to-do."

Peggy gripped the arm of the couch. How can she think I don't know that he's gone, she wondered. She stared at Mrs. Manning. "I know that."

Mrs. Manning had picked up a silver-framed photo. "This would not have happened if Wilbur had been here. In those days the boy always found a replacement before he left. It was very inconsiderate of Sing to leave so abruptly, very inconsiderate indeed."

She's pretending she didn't fire him, Peggy raged inwardly. She remembered Mum's comments about pinning down a piece of jelly. She swallowed.

"Did you fire him because he came to see our puppet show?"

Mrs. Manning set the photo down very carefully on the table and straightened up posture-perfect, really looking at Peggy for the first time. "I had to let him go, yes. I had no choice."

"But it was *my* fault. I asked him to come. I wanted him to be there. He helped us with the puppets and everything.

And it was only half an hour.'' Peggy heard her voice crack on the final words.

Mrs. Manning rearranged the doilies on the arms of her chair. Her hands trembled slightly.

"The point, Peggy dear, is disobedience. The houseboy shares my home. He has to be trustworthy." She reached over and patted Peggy's knee. Her hand felt hard, like a claw. "But it wasn't your fault. Don't worry about that."

Peggy stood up. In a loud sharp voice she didn't know, she said, "Stop it. Stop treating me like a little kid. It's not true. He didn't share your house. He just shared your crummy basement. And, anyway, he's not a boy. He's a *grown up man.*"

Peggy's words hung in the air. She felt a huge bubble sob rising in her throat and she turned to run away. As she turned, her vision cleared and she glanced at Mrs. Manning. Her brain took a snapshot. The old woman sat motionless. Her hands on the chair arms were gnarled and spotted with brown. Sunlight through the window lit her from behind, and there was a fine sprinkling of pink face powder on her glasses. Peggy fled down the dark hall and crashed out the front door.

The whirr of the lawnmower floated over from her house. Colin must be out cutting the grass. Peggy turned down the street, around two corners into the alley, and into the garage. She pulled open the back door of the car and collapsed on the seat. She was filled with the weak hollow sickness she always felt after losing her temper — the feeling of having been invaded and taken over by a stranger. She leaned forward and rested her head against the front seat. And this wasn't like getting mad at Colin or Linda Hoskins. This was yelling at a grownup. *And* an elderly grownup. *And* a member of the church. Mrs. Manning would complain to Dad and then Dad would give her heck. But worse than

110

that, it had all been useless. She didn't know anything more about Sing than she knew before.

She ripped the barrettes out of her hair. What good were barrettes and being respectful and polite and all the other things that pleased adults? Just saying the truth right out didn't seem to work, either.

Suddenly the garage felt chilly. Peggy wrapped herself in the car blanket and curled up on the seat. Soon she was asleep.

16

For a few days Peggy kept expecting to be called into Dad's office for a talking-to. But it didn't happen. Apparently Mrs. Manning was just going to ignore the whole thing. Peggy was relieved but also a bit disappointed. She had all her arguments ready and she was looking forward to using them. So finally she used them up on George, telling him the whole story. As she described Mrs. Manning and her house and what had happened, she gradually felt better. It wasn't one of those adventure stories where the kids solve everything and the bad guys are brought to justice. But she had done something hard and right, and maybe that was enough of an ending.

And then it was nearly September. Peggy went school-supplies shopping with Dorrie, and somewhere between pencil cases and binders she realized that she was actually looking forward to the beginning of school. The summer had gone limp and gluey. She wanted the crispness of new notebooks and leaves underfoot and the edge of cold in the morning air. George had told her once that when he was learning English he got the words "spring" and "fall" mixed up. She understood why. Spring was damp and warm and you just wanted to fall into it. Fall made you want to bend your knees, take a deep breath and spring into a new life.

She barely thought about Linda Hoskins until Mum brought her up one morning at breakfast.

"The Hoskins family have invited us to a Labour Day picnic."

Dad drained his big breakfast teacup, placed it firmly in the saucer and frowned. He stuck his chin out just the way Dorrie did in arguments. "I'm not going."

"But, honey, it's just a picnic. There will be lots of people there. It's not as if you would have to cope with Harry undiluted."

"He'll corner me, all the same. And then he'll regale me with off-colour stories, all the time waiting for me to look shocked, just so that he can dismiss the clergy as a bunch of prigs. He's a menace."

Peggy looked up in surprise. She knew that kids did that sort of thing to clergy kids, especially to Colin. But she hadn't known that grownups did it to Dad. More and more she seemed to be discovering that children and adults were much the same. This thought made her a bit tired. Maybe it didn't get easier.

"... and a terribly hard worker." Mum refilled Dad's cup. "We would never have gotten the church hall painted in the summer if it hadn't been for Harry Hoskins. Anyway, I know for a fact that Miss Blatherwick is coming. You can always talk dahlias with her."

Dad groaned the soft groan of defeat.

"And, Peggy? You're invited too, of course." Mum looked at her inquiringly. "We'd like it if you would come."

Peggy thought for a moment. "Okay."

The Hoskins had set up their backyard with trestle tables covered in bed sheets. Mr. Hoskins had put his portable hi-fi on the hood of his car and was handing out bottles of beer from a cooler in the trunk. "Hi, Reverend, how about a brew from my travelling bar?"

Mum became quickly absorbed in a group of women in the kitchen. Vats of potato salad and green jellied salad and

113

Parker House rolls and cold fried chicken began emerging in a steady stream. Linda was nowhere to be seen.

Peggy joined the human chain of bowls and platters and plates. She heard someone say, "Isn't she the helpful one?" and thought how being helpful was the perfect escape. She noticed Miss Blatherwick sitting on a deck chair, surrounded by the hubbub but alone. She had a bright smile on her face.

That's the "I'm feeling left out but I don't want anyone to feel sorry for me" smile, thought Peggy. The deck chair was low slung, and Miss Blatherwick did not look comfortable. She cast occasional looks toward the kitchen, from which the sound of busyness and hilarity emerged.

Peggy set down a plate of radish roses and cheese-stuffed celery, helped herself to an Orange Crush and went to sit on the grass beside Miss Blatherwick. A simple "hello" was enough to set Miss Blatherwick talking, and Peggy let the waves of words roll over her as she looked around the yard. The oasis of mown lawn with its chairs and tables was surrounded by a border of half-finished projects — a star-shaped flower bed filled with weeds, part of a dismantled car, a picket fence with pickets missing, a pile of bricks, a rusting swing set leaning at an angle, a doorless fridge.

More people arrived, more coolers, baskets, babies, lawn chairs. Mr. Hoskins turned up the volume on the hi-fi and began to line up beer bottles on the roof of his car. Dad came over to talk to Miss Blatherwick.

Mrs. Hoskins' arm shot out the back door, propelling Linda by the shoulder. Linda was wearing a frilly party dress, blue with white dots, with short puffy sleeves, a white plastic belt, and a crinoline that made the skirt stand away from her body like a bell. She walked stiffly down the stairs as though she was trying to prevent her dress from touching her. She was scowling, pale beneath her freckles, and even her elbows looked pointed and mean.

She plunked down on the grass beside Peggy, her crinoline bunching up on her lap. She punched it down.

"I *hate* this dress. My mother made me wear it."

"I think it's sort of pretty," said Peggy.

"It's *not*. It's *stupid*. Look at everyone else."

Peggy looked around at the cotton skirts and sleeveless blouses, at the bermuda shorts and at her own green striped pedal pushers. Nobody else was wearing party clothes.

"Maybe you can change later."

"Oh, yeah. When hell freezes over."

Peggy was shocked. Kids weren't allowed to say "hell," except when they all got to say it together and very loud in the choral recitation of "The Cremation of Sam McGee." She had also never heard of hell freezing. She smiled as she thought about the little flames turning to ice and the devil wearing a scarf and mittens.

"Well, it's not funny." Linda stood up and flounced off.

Peggy pursued her around the side of the garage. "I'm sorry. I wasn't laughing at you. I hate it too, when I'm wearing the wrong things and everybody looks at me. My mum won't let me wear nylons to school, even in grade seven. Will yours?"

Linda perked up and the conversation rolled along the well-worn path of perfectly reasonable things that your parents are too mean to let you do. When Mr. Hoskins called, "Chow time!" they went to sit at the same table.

During the meal Mr. Hoskins' voice got louder and louder. He kept standing up proposing toasts, and the other adults started to look uncomfortable. Once Mrs. Hoskins put her hand on his arm as he was standing up, but he just threw it off and looked really snarly for a second. He quieted down for a while and the general hum of the party continued. But again over cake and ice cream he started to talk about his children.

"Yup, before you know it, they are all grown up. Right, Marge?" Mrs. Hoskins gave a bright nod. "Why, even Linda, our youngest. Just the other day, so it seems, we were changing her diapers and now, well, she's a real young lady. Know what she got for her birthday?"

Peggy heard Linda beside her give a small gasp. She looked over and Linda was bent close to her plate, shovelling in her food.

"A brassiere, that's what. Well, I said to Marge, that's fine, Marge, but you'd better get a couple of grapefruits to go with it." Then Mr. Hoskins started to laugh, a loud laugh like a donkey. A one-beat pause followed his words, and then the conversation rushed in again, a little desperately at first and then flowing as before.

Peggy glanced toward Linda without moving her head. Linda continued to shovel cake into her mouth, not looking up. Peggy flailed around in her mind for something to say and grabbed a question at random. "So. Who do you want for home room this year? Miss Eshom or Mrs. Kerr?"

After some vigorous swallowing, Linda expressed her strong opinions on both choices. Then they talked about what they were going to wear the first day of school. Linda had new babydoll wedgies. Peggy had new saddle oxfords, as usual. She pretended to complain about them — "Even if I *was* allowed to wear nylons, who'd wear them with corny old saddle oxfords!" Linda wanted to wear a felt circle skirt and hoped the weather wouldn't be too hot.

They did not talk about fathers or horses, about lying or arithmetic tests. Everything that had happened the previous spring seemed an endless summer ago.

17

A ND then it was the first day of school. Peggy walked down the hill, concentrating on keeping her feet flat so as not to crack the tops of the new black and white saddle oxfords. Her cotton blouse felt crisp and cool and smelled like sunshine. George whizzed by on his bike. His briefcase was tied onto the carrier with a thick piece of rope. He waved over his shoulder as he passed. Peggy grinned.

As the roar of the schoolyard became louder and the green frame building appeared, she waited for the familiar sick, suffocating feeling. But when she saw the knot of girls around the dramatically gesturing Linda, she couldn't really remember why they had seemed so scary. Jane saw her and waved. Linda waved too, and yelled in her megaphone voice, "Hey, Peggy, come on over!"

As she approached the group Peggy noticed a new girl leaning against the gym wall, peering at her fingernails. She glanced away. But then she remembered her own first day.

I think I'll say hello, she thought, surprising herself. But what could she say that wouldn't sound dumb? Her feet slowed, kicking up gravel as she crossed the field. Then the answer came to her. Act like a puppet. Puppets said dumb and obvious things all the time, just to get the story moving. And that's what conversation with a new person was really about, after all, just getting the story moving.

So she took a deep breath and walked over to the new girl.

"Hi, you must be new. My name's Peggy. What grade are you in?" Between that curtain-raiser and the school buzzer ten minutes later, Peggy made three discoveries. First of all it turned out that the new girl, whose name was Arabella, had just moved from the country as well. Second, when Linda and the group wandered over and Peggy introduced Arabella, it seemed that all the prickles and meanness of the previous spring had disappeared. Third, and best of all, Peggy discovered that you didn't have to be a puppet for too long. Somewhere around the four-minute mark, Peggy the puppet and Peggy the person melted into each other.

Being a puppet helped Peggy through some tricky things that fall. When she had to give an oral report on the making of plywood, she was a public-speaking puppet. When a bus driver wouldn't believe that she was only twelve and tried to make her pay full adult fare, she stood up to him, a puppet in the right. At the Parish Harvest Dance she couldn't quite manage being a dancing puppet, but she did hand out cups of tea and talk to people that she didn't know.

With the help of her various puppet disguises, Peggy got to know more about the kids in grade seven. She found out that Donna Parfitt had diabetes and that Dwayne McVitie's father was a professional wrestler. She learned that Harriet Carruthers had a disaster story for every season, from the pumpkin candles that set the house on fire, to how nail polish makes your fingernails fall off, to the poisoned turkey stuffing that wiped out a whole family. The class stopped being a blur and became a group of real people with budgies, revolting brothers and plantar warts.

The months went by and the windows of the primary school changed their decorations from leaves to pumpkins to poppies to Santas to snowflakes.

"Hey, did you use to make snowflakes in grade one?" Peggy asked Jane. "Remember how it seemed like magic when they turned out?"

118

It was the first week back to school in January. A green Christmas had been followed by a deep white New Year's, and Peggy and Jane were trudging up the hill home from school.

"Mine usually just turned into confetti," Jane replied. "I wasn't a very good cutter-outer in grade one. But in grade two they got me leftie scissors and then I could do anything, even those daffodils with stick-up middles."

They were passing Mrs. Manning's house, and Peggy got one of her odd flash memories of Sing, of the scissors flying as silhouettes appeared from the paper. She tilted her head back and tried to catch snowflakes on her tongue.

"Look! Nobody's messed up your front lawn yet." Jane pulled open the gate. "Let's make snow angels."

They were so wet and cold after lying in the snow that Peggy had to lend Jane a set of clothes. She was staying for dinner as she often did on Thursday nights when her mother worked late.

At dinner Dad tried to interest everyone in the article he had been reading on the Great Wall of China. But he didn't have much luck. Colin kept interrupting to talk about his motorcycle. Peggy and Jane were giggling because Nebbie-cat was on Peggy's lap, hidden by the overhanging table-cloth, a fact they were trying to conceal. Even Dorrie, usually a good listener, was distracted. She kept slipping a card out of her pocket and looking at it.

"What's that?" asked Colin.

"It's the periodic table of the elements. I'm memorizing atomic numbers."

"Ah, yes," said Dad. "Dorrie's eleventh commandment, 'Thou shalt not waste time.'"

"That's a pretty weird thing to memorize," said Colin.

"Well, at least I have something useful in my head," retorted Dorrie.

"Hey! I've got useful things in my head. I know all about pickles, for example. I know, as a matter of fact, the entire periodic table of pickles. You've got your dills, they're a seventeen. Then you've got your gherkins, they're a three. Then of course there's your special mixed with extra cauliflower, a solid eight." Colin winked at Jane, who giggled.

"How about the valences of vegetables?" said Dad.

Mum rolled her eyes. "This is one of those conversations that convinces me that I am not related to any of you. You must all be changelings, and that goes for you too, Gareth." She passed the pudding to Jane. "Does your family go on this way?"

Jane grinned and shrugged. "Not really. But I like it."

The doorbell rang. Dad sighed and half-rose.

"No, it's okay," said Dorrie, "it's probably Charles. We're going out." Charles was Dorrie's boyfriend. She had met him at university, in a chemistry class.

"Ah, yes," said Colin, "the romantic scent of hydrogen sulfide, the subdued light of the bunsen burner. It was inevitable."

But Dorrie returned with a package and a puzzled expression. "Parcel post. It's for Peggy."

Peggy took it. What could it be? Not a late Christmas present. She had had her fancy soap from Aunt Flora, her *Girls Own Annual* from England and her mitts and scarf from the prairies. She hadn't sent away for anything. It was too early for even a very early birthday present.

Mum was equally intrigued. "What's the postmark? Dawson Creek? Do we know anyone in Dawson Creek?"

Peggy opened the parcel to reveal a letter and several small packages wrapped in red paper. The letter was written in thin, careful handwriting. She read it aloud.

Dear Peggy,

Sing Lee asked me to write to you and send you news. My name is Cathy and I live with my father and my

120

uncle and aunt here in Dawson Creek. My uncle knew Sing many years ago and when he saw his picture in the paper he remembered him and was sorry that he had lost touch. So he wrote to some friends in Vancouver and they knew where Sing was. He told us that he was not working and my uncle asked if he would like to come here where we have a store and a hotel. So he did. He says to tell you that he is sorry that he did not say goodbye to you and that he thinks of you and your family and George often. Also the cat (whose name I can't spell!). He sends these small presents to wish you a Happy New Year and he hopes that one day he will see you again. This is the end of Sing's message. But I feel like I know you because your picture from the paper is on our wall and because Sing talks a lot about you. It sounds like you had lots of fun.

Yours sincerely,
Cathy Yung

Peggy fought the lump in her throat, handed the letter to Mum and began to investigate the packages. A flat thin one for Dad, a square one for Mum, a chocolate-boxy one for the whole family and a rattly one for her. But the largest one was labelled "George."

"I'd better phone him." George answered the phone. He and Peggy didn't see each other as much as they had over the summer, with Peggy in the band and George in the chess club. But they still talked nearly every day.

"Hey, George, get on over here. Secret surprise."

The rattle and clink of a bicycle on the front porch announced George's arrival.

"He rides his bike in the snow? Just to come next door?" asked Jane.

"He rides his bike *everywhere*," said Peggy.

When George read the letter he became very quiet for a moment. Then they opened the packages in turn.

Dad had silk handkerchiefs. Mum had tea in a blue and white tin. The whole family had candied ginger. Peggy opened her parcel carefully and lifted a paper-wrapped object out of a light wood box. It was a mobile made of small squares of glass, each painted with a different flower. She blew on it and it tinkled.

George's present was the heaviest. Inside the parcel, all fitted together like a puzzle, were boxes of fireworks. There were rockets, pinwheels, Roman candles, lawn fountains, star shells, Catherine wheels and the mysteriously named extra-large python snake. The labels were decorated with birds and animals, temples, bridges and flower maidens.

"Well, George," said Dad with a twinkle in his eye, "I suppose you'll want to save these for Halloween."

"I could," said George, who understood about Dad's teasing, "but I think these are Chinese New Year fireworks and they might get stale."

"We certainly wouldn't want that," said Dad. "Shall we set them off tonight?"

The church garden wasn't big enough, so they did it on their front lawn. Mum got out all the summer deck chairs from the basement and set them up on the front porch with blankets and quilts. Dad admitted to a lifelong terror of fireworks, so George and Colin were in charge. Mr. and Mrs. Slobodkin came and Jane phoned her mother to come after work. Charles arrived and after some serious discussion, he and Dorrie decided to skip their lecture on bivalves of the Pacific coast.

The first explosion made the across-the-alley dog begin to bark, and soon people started appearing. Heads poked out windows, front doors opened and porches started to fill up. A line of people formed at the front fence. Mum poured cocoa from thermoses, and Old Billy from the rooming house three doors down started circulating his bottle of rye.

A light flicked on in a window next door. Peggy looked and saw Mrs. Manning holding aside a lace curtain, and peering up into the sky. Mr. Slobodkin came by with a mug of cocoa for Peggy. When she looked again the curtains had fallen closed.

The sky filled with flowers of light. The Murphys, who hadn't gotten around to taking down their Christmas lights, switched them on again and the tiny spots of colour reflected the grand explosions in the sky above. Colin and George began to set off two things at once, and the colours mingled and fell together. In the moment of the fireworks heading whooshing into the sky everyone held their breath and let it all out in an ''ahhhh'' together. The display ended with the sinuous writhings of the extra-long python snake, and then George went around with sparklers for everyone, even throwing them up to people at windows. The Murphy kids twirled theirs in hoola hoops of light until they fell over in the snow. The grownups stuck theirs in the window boxes and in the fences.

Peggy saved hers for a moment, lit it from the glowing end of Colin's and took it around to the side of the house. She tried to write her name, but the P faded before she got to the second G.

Her sparkler began to sputter and another light joined it as George stepped up beside her. He sketched a square with a line through it in the air. ''Remember that?'' It was the Chinese character for moon.

''Quick! Do it again,'' said Peggy.

And together they wrote in the air — George the character for moon, Peggy the character for sun — together making ''bright.'' And bright it glowed, green in the air for a moment, before dissolving into the night.